CRYPTIC ENCOUNTERS

Conceptualized By

ENAKSHI J

# INKQUILLS®

Published by InkQuills Publishing House
www.inkquills.in

First Edition 2020
All Rights Reserved. Copyright © 2020
ISBN: 978-81-945636-2-4

FOREWORD

Among the many remarkable things that have happened to worldwide literature in recent years, one of the most significant is how horror has crept back onto the shelves of the readers and has even become mainstream. Until a few decades ago, horror was considered to be the poor cousin of other literary genres, the black sheep of the family so to say, or the one chipped cup in the set that was never brought out for the guests. The best places to pick up a horror novel were in the seedy corner shops or drugstores or in secondhand markets, and even then, there wasn't much of a choice. Readers of the genre had to make do with the titles and authors that were peddled to them. But now we are on a brink of an explosion of the genre. With large publishing houses banking on horror and bookstores and literature festivals giving prime placement to horror authors, the genre is certainly on an upswing.

The factors that have precipitated this change are too many to get into here. We can talk about the resurgence of the genre on screen which has trickled down to literature, or that more authors are considering writing speculative fiction, or that the world has finally acknowledged the fact that some of the most enduring literary works are in the horror genre, even to the extent of including classic horror novels in academic curricula. But I'd like to put the onus of the popularity of the horror genre squarely on the readers.

The contemporary reader is well-exposed to many literary works from around the world. They have read diverse stories across genres. As such, the same old-fashioned storytelling tropes do not hold their interest any longer. The modern reader wants to explore new realms of storytelling and challenge their own analytical ability as they read. Stories need to be unique and different and trigger that part of their brain that does not just receive information from the stories they read, but examines it deeply and enjoys being affected by it. This is where the horror genre works beautifully.

We often think that horror stories are merely restricted to ghosts and spirits. While the paranormal is a strong element in horror, the genre goes much beyond that, and contemporary horror fiction has proved it. Several subgenres of horror coexist on the bookshelves now, including and not limited to gore, supernatural, fantasy, psychological, urban legends and folklore, among others. Of course, the ghosts and spirits haven't gone anywhere, but it is also true that many horror stories of today aren't speculative but are set in the real world with real people and no fantastical elements whatsoever. And these factors have given rise to an entire new legion of horror readers, who is a more astute reader than their predecessors of the genre.

Evoking fear is deeply psychological in nature, which is why I believe that all horror writers have an innate understanding of the machinations of the human mind. It is a prerequisite for the job. This understanding reflects in their work. A horror story may not have supernatural elements—it may be a story of a serial killer or of a phobia or perhaps just about a lonely ride on a long highway at night—but they will all have one common element; the element of dread that's born in the mind of the protagonist and, hence, the reader.

And, thus, we come to talk about this anthology that I have the privilege to write this foreword for. *Cryptic Encounters* checks all the right horror boxes with its thirteen stories, and, what's more, it goes beyond the norm to explore new areas. The stories in here all adhere to a theme—that of meeting someone (or something) unexpected, and the chain of sequences that unfold.

I read somewhere recently that of all the people we come across in public, there are several who might not be what we think they are. They could be spirits of people who have died, or people from other dimensions, or aliens masquerading as us. Who knows? They might be innocuously walking amongst us for reasons best known to them. We might be actually walking with ghosts and meeting and interacting with them without realizing it. But, even keeping the paranormal aside, haven't we all had chance encounters with people who have altered our day and perhaps even our lives?

The stories in here are about such encounters. One of the things I enjoyed immensely about the stories was how different they were from style and execution, which is understandable given that they come from writers from across the globe. The distinct flavor each individual writer brings to the stories is what makes this book a worthy collection for true aficionados of horror.

If you are a reader who doesn't take things at face value but likes to get deeper into the subtext and examine, then you will surely enjoy these tales. In a time when horror is getting its due recognition, this collection is one more noteworthy attempt in boosting the genre, and therein lies its biggest achievement.

~Neil D'Silva

(Author of *Maya's New Husband, Yakshini, Haunted*)

EDITOR'S NOTE

An eerie sound often echoes near me

But the moment I try to identify

The mere sight makes me cry,

For the unusual sight is bizarre and uncommon

However much I try, my mind has thoughts I cannot shun!

These cryptic encounters

Make my blood run cold

People say that I hallucinate a lot

They refuse to believe the notions my mind has caught.

We meet a lot of people on a daily basis but seldom do we pause and try to initiate a conversation with them. While most of the encounters are forgotten immediately, some encounters leave us marked for life. They say that it is all in the mind and to some extent, this is true because your thoughts are the seeds that you plant in your mind. Eventually, these thoughts make you the victim and it becomes difficult to escape the clutches of fear and agony. Over time, we begin giving names to those invisible creatures that we feel around us. The most common of them being the Ghosts.

Ghosts are real. If you do not believe in the existence of the sad intangible beings who grieve and yearn, then you should know that ghosts are a part of our being too. Life is a balance of the good and the bad. Every individual has a good side as well as a bad side. Depending upon the circumstance, the mind reveals the face of the person. Hence, the existence of ghosts, whether inside or outside, is real, very real.

'Cryptic Encounters' is an attempt to bring forth stories based on paranormal activities, uncanny encounters with spirits, uncanny dreams turning into reality, diabolical mindset and precognition. Such encounters cannot be forgotten easily. Some of these stories are true experiences of the authors and some of them are just a figment of their imagination. Nevertheless, each one of them is different and is sure to linger in your mind for long.

Collating the best works by authors across the globe, this anthology will definitely give you goosebumps. The stories express varied emotions ranging from sorrow, guilt, fear to anger, hatred and hope. These stories are just to entertain the readers and not mock any faith, religion or belief. Accompanying each story is a quatrain that I have composed to add to the eeriness of the atmosphere.

I thank all the contributing authors for being a part of this project and using their talent to contribute to the world of entertainment. I would also like to thank Shannon E. Gardner for providing such beautiful illustrations. They definitely act like the icing on the cake.

~Enakshi J.

(Editor of *Poison Ivy* and *Unbounded Trajectories*)

CONTRIBUTING WRITERS

I walk up and down the empty house

Only to find the vacant room and your invisible presence,

The more I try to ignore my wailing spouse,

The more the cries make me feel farther from heavens.

CRIES
~Alan Derosby~

I hear the cries, the ones that wake me up from my deep sleep. They are loud, low cries like the sound of a baby. I lean over to tell my wife to go check on Sammy, our little boy, but decide against sending her. It is easier if I check myself. Once I hear it, I'm awake anyway. No need to make others miss vital sleep time.

When I get out of bed, I slide my robe on, hiding a body that is more and more emaciated with every passing day. I had stopped eating at first due to a lack of hunger. Now I can barely hold anything down. It's as if my body is rejecting any kind of nourishment, wanting to end this terror. I tie the robe, dragging my feet across the cold wooden floor. The chill of the winter months against my skin sends a wave of cold through me, waking me up just that much more. I close the bedroom door behind me, keeping the chill of the night air locked inside.

The cries become louder, first a soft moan before breaking into a scream. I rush down the hallway, not even turning on the light before reaching my son's room. I open the door expecting to see him sitting up, his face wet with tears and eyes red and puffy, but there's no movement in his bed. I walk over to the edge of his bed, laying my hand on his pillow, not wanting to wake him. I don't know where the noise is coming from, the same as most nights. It's as if his cries stop when I enter the room. Maybe knowing I am close by is enough to put lovely Sam back to sleep. I first sit and then lay on the end of his bed holding my robe tight against me for warmth. I won't get into his covers or grab one of his blankets out of the closet. I'd rather not wake him.

I fall asleep, waking up hours later. It is still dark, though I wish the sun were up. I slowly drag myself back into my room, closing his and then my bedroom door. I quietly take my robe off my body, hanging it on my bedpost. When I slide back under my covers, I make sure not to disrupt anything. I am lucky I received a bit of rest in my son's room because as soon as I close my eyes, I hear the screams again. They aren't for any one person, but I know I need to answer the call. I get out of bed, rush down the hallway into Sam's room and look inside. There is no sound coming from the place at all except the silence of a young son. The noises don't stop. They are coming from down in the living room. It is no longer the cries of a child woken from a nightmare but the sounds of a woman screaming in pain. I forget to tie my robe, running down the steps and into the sizable windowless room that I once called the Grand Room. Though it has a television and all the necessary items for a comfortable, relaxing environment, I no longer use it. It is more of a reminder of the past and not the place I wish to spend any more time than I have to. I want to sit on the couch but don't dare to. The noises have gone back to cries; I rush back upstairs to have a look again. The screams and cries bounce off one another, much like it does every night. I hate the darkness of the nights.

I finally decide to go back to my own bed, turning on all the lights so I can read. I can hear the cries and screams coming from the other rooms. I try to bury my face in a book but it is of no use. I want to yell for the noise to stop, but it does no good. I've tried everything, but I'm alone in this battle. There is no one to turn to when I want help.

Eventually, the pills kick in and I fall asleep amongst all the turmoil. When I awake later in the day, the house is filled with silence. I don't need to worry about waking up for a job. I lost it years back, unable to keep a schedule. It started with a few late arrivals. My boss understood the condition but he was running a business and my tardiness became too much of an issue. Now, sitting at my kitchen table with a cup of black coffee, I bury my head in my hands, zoning into nothingness. I know the cries will return the following evening.

I go into my son's room, the room he once slept in, played in and died in. Cancer seems to have no care as to race, religion, sexual orientation, or age. Death came for him one evening as he lay in his bed. My wife and I refused to let him die in a hospital. Instead, we surrounded him by people who truly loved him. I held his hand as he slipped away. Now he cries for me at night though I can't help him. Two years later, my wife took her own life. She decided to gulp an entire bottle of pills, washing them down with a fifth glass of vodka. I found her when I returned from work. She left no note but held my son's picture against her breast. Each evening, she returns, screaming to the Heavens about the child that was taken away.

I have no idea about my mental state. My doctor says it's my way of dealing with death, but I think otherwise. When I lay on my son's bed, though I refuse to move a single sheet out of place, I can feel his calm love as if I held him again. My wife, however, is a different story. She screams at night, never stopping, crying out to the one person she still desires. No embraces or hugs can quell the rage of a mother's loss.

Purring in the streets so dark,

I wander leaving behind many a mark.

It is not just me but many others alike

Who roam about aimlessly and are ghost-like!

THE SCREAM
~Avijit Roy~

'Papa, get up, I need to go to the washroom to pee,' said nine-year-old Leno. He then pushed his father, Brando, who was lying open-mouthed with air whistling in and gurgling out. It was a tough challenge for Leno to get a sound sleep lying beside his father.

The clock struck twelve with its scary pendulum scolding the stubborn ticking of the machine on the wall.

'Papa, get up.' When Leno pushed his father harder this time, it was a little fruitful as Brando groaned and rolled back onto the other side.

Sleep was rooted in his eyes like leeches, persistent and invincible.

'Papa.'

'Huh, yea, I'm up now, boy.' Brando stretched out his limbs to clear out the lingering laziness.

'I need to go pee,' Leno repeated like it was a verse of a hymn.

When Leno was done in the washroom, his father said, 'Go to bed. I will flush for you.'

The warm bed was very welcoming to the drooping figure of the boy. Crumpling like a piece of paper, he waited for his father to join him. The sleep was now sluggish to infect his eyes.

After a few minutes, when Leno moved his fingers around, he felt the empty space, ascertaining that his father hadn't returned. He didn't care for the moment. The night had devoured all other sounds except that of the clock.

'Papa, are you back?'

Receiving no reply, Leno called out to his father again but didn't receive any response. He became conscious that his father hadn't returned from the washroom. Leno sent out a loud call towards the washroom which was inches away from their bedroom, 'Papa, how long will you take? I'm alone.' He swallowed the words that could have expressed his fear lest his father would make fun of him and then it would reach his friends' ears.

Not a single word agitated the air and by then fear had burdened Leno's heart.

'Papa, is this a joke that…' Leno was startled half way into his speech by the loud banging of the clock's pendulum announcing that it was half past twelve.

'Papa, please come out,' Leno cried out as tears started to moisten his eyelids.

Silence. Leno's heart pounded upon his ribs as if it was fit to burst. A mild breeze dared to push the door, making the hinges produce a screeching sound. He struggled to breathe.

He had never slept alone since his mother had passed away two years ago. At that moment, he felt the loneliest. Sleep had bidden adieu to his physic and as he put his trembling feet onto the floor, it pricked his sole like icy arrows that can only be felt inside a grave. The chill was injected into his bones.

'Papa, it's not fair to joke at such a time. Please come out.' Leno urged fighting tears but the tears had decided to roll down anyway.

He inched forward and held the door. A thought that his father might be just behind the door playing hide and seek was a very irrational proposition, but it really made its way into his brain. He pulled open the door with a sudden jerk in order to catch his father. No one was there. *Had his father evaporated into the air?* He didn't let that spooky thought rule over him.

Leno braved forward towards the door, which, to his surprise, was not locked.

'Papa?' Leno called out softy before he ventured to push the door open. Obviously, no answer came to appease his tension.

'Papa, are you alright?' Leno asked meekly as another thought, more rational this time, hit his brain. *What if father had an accident!* That scenario also seemed possible. He pushed the door but it didn't yield to his restrained effort. Wind passed whispering by his ears.

'Who's that?' Leno stammered as he turned back to face a weird figure. He must have been disappointed because it was only air and a dark wall behind him.

His brain was crammed with fear and an urge to get rid of it pulled him inside the washroom which was empty of any human presence.

'Papa?' Leno screamed, 'Where are you?'

His words echoed with a gravity of a howling animal. He had to stuff his ears so that he couldn't hear other sounds. The washroom was a six feet square enclosure that had no other way out. He couldn't believe that the whole mass of his father's body had magically vanished. The silence was growing around like a thick fog and Leno felt suffocated.

'Papa!' was Leno's last call before he fainted and fell on the floor.

Leno lay on the floor with his limbs sprawled for half an hour. His senses were still imprisoned in oblivion.

Then a voice from an invisible source whispered in his unconscious ears, 'Leno, wake up,' and a shiver animated his apparently lifeless body. He struggled to open his eyelids that, like heavy iron plates, revolted against his effort. The darkness was smeared on his vision. For once he thought that it was his father calling him out of his sleep but later realized that the voice was only a figment of his imagination.

The silence was now diluted with the dripping sound of the tap water. The clock hadn't even crossed the space of fifteen seconds when the chilling memory of his father's mysterious disappearance returned and he shuddered. A street lamp, four yards away, had illuminated the overhead square window like a lit-up television screen. The light was filtering in through foliage of some twisted branches outside and some macabre shadows were painted on the wall inside the washroom. Leno figured that they looked like a witch with spiky fingers and sharp nails. It was all a child's imagination! Words were entangled in Leno's throat, but he retrieved his cry, 'Papa, where are you?'

Gathering some courage, he got up and craned his neck to peek through the window and look for a rescuer but to his dismay, his eyes met no such living soul around. It was so late in the night that he couldn't hope for a better result.

His attention fell on the tap that was still dripping and as he stared at the liquid, he perceived in the faint light that it seemed reddish. Showing his bravery, he extended his trembling hand to clear his doubt. The liquid felt thicker as a drop fell on his open palm. He moved his hand towards the window light and discovered that it was a drop of blood.

'Papa,' he let out a weird sound in spite of knowing that his father was nowhere around. He became desperate to get out of that surrounding. He darted out of the washroom and then through the bedroom towards the door which was still latched from inside.

In the next instant, he moved out of the house and ended up in the lane crying for help. It felt as if he was in a cemetery because only the whisking wind gave him company.

'Is anybody there? Please help me. Is anybody awake?' His deafening calls were consumed by thick shrubbery around.

Suddenly a meowing from behind startled him. Leno, like a top turning on its orbit, faced two phosphorus eyes of a ghastly black cat which added a new dimension to his horror. He rolled back on his feet and tripped on a stone but he didn't lose his balance. Then came plenty of cats meowing from every neighboring house that lined the lane. A few cats came down the lanes, some from the stairs of the houses and some more were peering out of the doors and the windows.

Cats were everywhere and each one was identical black. Leno started to run down the winding lane. Exhausted and drenched in perspiration, he realized that he hadn't progressed even a yard. The experience scared the daylights out of him!

The cats were swarming from every corner like bees into a hive. Their eyes were burning bright and their meow was terrifying.

'Leno, my boy.'

A nebulous figure came out tearing through the darkness. The faded body and the voice confirmed that it was his father.

'Papa!' Leno rushed towards him with stretched hands.

'No, stop. Don't come near me.'

Leno was surprised; he didn't understand what was up with his father.

'Why, Papa? Look, the black cats are present everywhere and they will scratch me to death.'

'Don't worry, my boy,' his father assured, 'they won't harm you. Now, I am one of them. The whole village is a cat shelter.'

A deep frown was evident on Leno's forehead.

'Yes,' his father resumed, 'this village has no living human beings. They all have metamorphosed into black cats. Every night it happens with one or the other. Tonight, it was my turn.' Saying that, the father's shadowy figure stepped closer to Leno and the harrowing sight of the furry face, grey eyes and hairy moustache caught Leno off guard. 'In some time, you, too, will be transformed.'

Leno's bulged eyes seemed to spring out of their sockets. His face flashed fear and he indeed believed that it was a metaphysical world woven around him where he was the only human survivor.

'Come Leno, it's our own world.'

Slowly but steadily his father's figure shrank down to a perfect feline structure that made a loud meowing sound.

'No…,' Leno woke up with the scream. The night hadn't yielded to the sunlight yet. He breathed a sigh of relief when he realized that it was a dream. He reached out to locate his father but instead felt the fur of the black cat that lay beside him, its eyes wide open, shining.

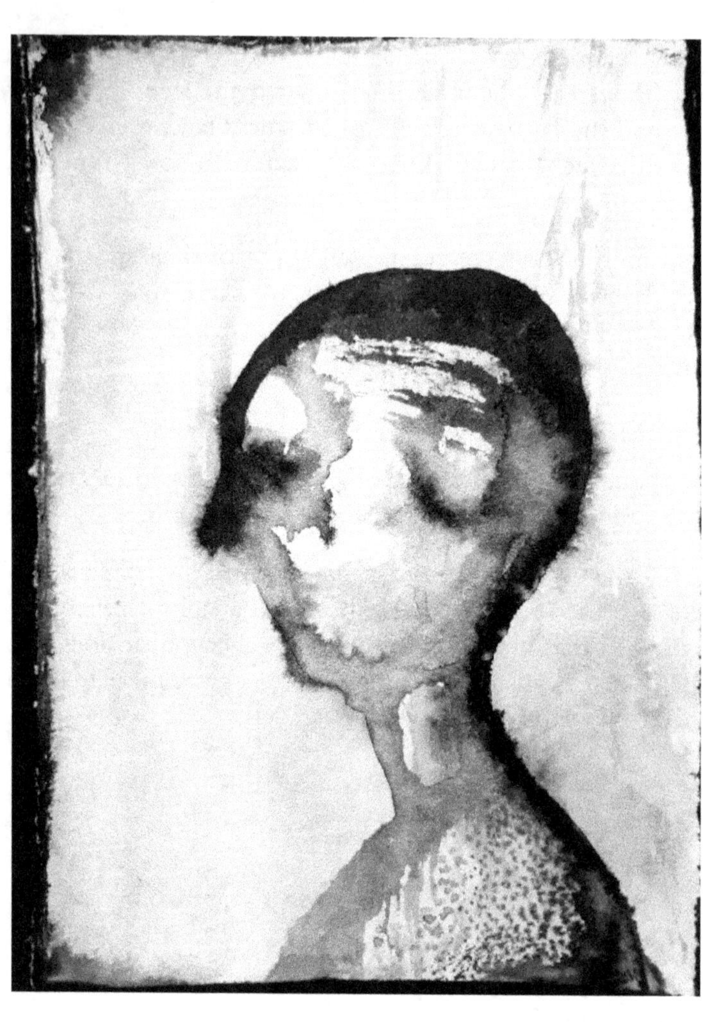

The cryptic encounter with the shadows so wild,

Often disturbs the mind and robs the soul.

It doesn't hurt nor is the body reviled

But it leaves you vacant and not the whole!

A NIGHT TO REMEMBER
~Biswadeep Ghosh Hazra~

The sun's rays fell on my face as if caressing me and teasing me at the same time. I tried shifting on my side but was surprised to feel water on my face. It took me a couple of minutes to figure out everything, and once I did, the only thing I could do was smile. Getting back to my senses was the easy part; it was getting up that proved to be difficult. I felt as if every joint and tendon, every bone and muscle in my body was clasped shut. I was like those tin-men that are bought as souvenirs, found in museums and antique shops, cursed to be frozen forever.

I eyed around and found myself to be in a familiar environment, albeit not at a proper time. I tried to inch up but couldn't; it was as if my torso was nailed to the ground and my legs had started sprouting roots of sorts. Angry at myself for not being able to perform a simple task of getting up, I let out a scream and tried to jerk myself up. The sudden force must have been too much to bear as I blacked out at the last moment; the last thing I remembered was the massive knock on the head and entering into a vortex-like structure. I could see the painful brightness on the other end.

---***---

'Are you okay, brother?' a familiar hand patted my back, his voice trailing off quite evidently. I motioned to him that I was alright. I knew I was not. I was drunk and couldn't make a head or toe of things.

'Breakups are always hard,' I heard Riju speaking. Between my incessant vomiting and drinking on top of the college roof, I was having the time of my life. We were celebrating my roommate's birthday and alcohol literally rained from the hostel roof. We were in our third year. Just another year and a half was left for the college to be over. That made us nostalgic.

Like Riju, a lot of friends came and went while I was purging my body of the poison.

As the moon hit high above our heads, my roommate rose up with great difficulty and proposed a toast. We were the kings of the night, enjoying ourselves and getting 'wasted'. We were like the Romans on the victory night- twenty-five to thirty odd teenagers from different parts of the country, enjoying the spoils of war.

---***---

Suddenly, amidst the hustle and bustle, someone shouted or more accurately mumbled something loudly. For a moment, we thought that the scumbag, our warden, had come to check our whereabouts, but as fate would have it, it was one of my friends. He wanted to narrate a Ghost story. I would be lying if I said that the ambience was not perfect. It really was. The dark of the night was lit only by the intermittent moonlight that peeped through the clouds. The distant howling of the foxes added to the eerie surrounding. Situated in the middle of a forest, our college often gave out spooky vibes that were enough to send a chill down the spine. There was dead silence as our narrator, Souvick, rose up on his feet with a little help from us.

Within a fraction of a second, Souvick's cheerful disposition changed into a serious one; his voice changed from laughing like a shy girl to a deep baritone which left all of us stunned. Thinking that he was creating the atmosphere for the narrative, I mentally applauded his effort. Finding good storytellers in an Engineering college was equivalent to finding a needle in a haystack. Thus, we all became quite excited at the prospect of listening to a great story.

'What I am about to tell you has happened in reality; hence, this is more of a memoir than a story,' Souvick said in a voice that could rival the legendary Amitabh Ji and we were left to stare at each other, drunk and visibly confused. Souvick continued, almost hypnotically, 'This hostel, where we are now, was made many moons ago on top of a graveyard.' The logical part of my brain went, 'Oh yes, the age-old graveyard below the hostel story,' but the other half wanted to believe him. It almost felt as if sinister hands were coming straight from the cement-laden roof, trying to snatch us. I was surrounded by Saahil, Riju and Aslam and I could feel the tension build within their bodies as Souvick went on with his delicious concoction of a horror story.

'Four years ago, on this very night, a boy committed suicide by jumping off this very roof. He lived on the third floor, in one of the rooms in the right wing…' I cut Souvick short by letting out a loud grunt and saying, 'Rubbish!' It did not matter though because others seemed quite immersed in Souvick's narration. My words intervened in their pleasure and they shot me a disgusted look.

'You all cannot fall for his cheap tricks in storytelling,' I protested but seeing that most of the people there wanted me to stop, I suppressed my angst. Souvick continued, 'Right, where were we? Yes, so his name was Ryan and he caught his girlfriend having sex with his best friend, who was also his roommate in the hostel.' Ours was not a co-ed hostel, in fact, no hostel in our college was, but people always found innovative ways to trick the law. Creativity ignites the mind when the stakes are exciting enough, I guess.

'One night, he bought the cheapest whiskey he could find, filled up his entire being with the poison and attached a rope to one of the pipes there…' Souvick paused to indicate the pipes and then continued with a grim expression.

'Now, at this point, it is important to mention that our roof has a network of pipes running through it with concrete supports in between. These pipes are made of metal and they are extremely durable. It is no wonder that one can easily tie a rope to these pipes and simply jump off the ledge of the roof.

The pipes are so strong that they will not move and the body can hang onto them for a long, long time!' The long pause was uncalled for but that forced my brain to start its functioning.

I was jerked back to the present with Souvick's booming voice. He continued, 'Ryan's body was found the next morning by the sweepers who are usually the first people to wake up. People say that his body was dangling right on top of our hostel insignia; it made an 'I' between the D and E'.' A cold rush traversed from my back to my head making me a bit dizzy. Souvick's explanation was indeed vivid, perhaps too vivid for our liking. The motto of our hostel was Deliverance Through Duty, and Ryan's body changed its meaning. It would have read something like D(I)ELIVERANCE. The mere thought of it sent shivers down my spine.

"Die"- the word played in my head on an endless loop. Was it a cruel game of irony and fate that made Ryan die the way he did? We may never know. That night, before we left, I heard our narrator say, 'I have heard that Ryan roams in our hostel premise late at night. You all should be a little careful.' His evil laugh gave out a sense of foreboding. It could have put Jack Nicholson from Shining to shame. And then, just with the click of a switch, Souvick was back to being his normal, cheery self.

It seemed as if someone possessed him long enough for the story to be told. I laughed at my judgmental thinking. How drunk and stoned I was to be thinking of such things!

---***---

Before heading to my room, I went to the place where Souvick said Ryan's body was found hanging. I peeked from the ledge in anticipation only to find a crow nesting on the sun shade beside the insignia. When I started walking towards the staircase, a strange sensation gripped me. My legs felt heavy and my head was dizzy. It was evident that I had had a little too much of both alcohol and smoke. College life was indeed wild. Somehow, I managed to reach my floor. My legs felt like jelly and I feared that they would collapse any moment. Something inside me urged me to use the common bathroom before going to my room. While all others headed straight to their rooms, I ended up taking wobbly strides towards the bathroom. Standing under the cold shower, I enjoyed every drop of water that caressed my body. The common bathroom had cubicle system wherein each cubicle was separated from the other through a wall that didn't reach up to the ceiling.

I do not remember how much time I spent in the shower; I remember I had the common sense to keep my mobile on top of the dividing wall to prevent it from getting wet. Being tall had its own set of advantages, I guess. But strangely enough, throughout the time my head was under the shower, I felt I was being watched by someone. I had a strange sensation that was hard to describe or write in words.

In that moment, I realized that as the cold water wiped off the intoxication from my head, it also made place for fear inside my head. I was scared. I was alone. Anxious that I was, I couldn't help but assume that I was being watched since the time I stepped onto the roof. Panicking a little, I ran my hand over the wall to get hold of my phone but to no avail. I tried brushing my hand on all the sides of the walls but still couldn't locate the phone.

Before I blacked out, my hand felt something as cold as ice, something that could not be explained with logic nor reason. The moment I touched it, I felt everything at once- anger, hate, sadness, joy, death. Yes, I felt death. It is said that curiosity often kills the cat. My curiosity to turn my head and find out what was lurking in the beyond tried to get the better of me. While my body refused to turn and give in, my mind relentlessly pushed my senses to meet with the other force. I could sense that there was someone perched on the wall that separated my cubicle from the rest. From the corner of my eye, I could make out that it resembled a human body. With hollow courage and a non-resistant body, I glanced at the figure. What

I saw was inexplainable, for it defied the realms of reasoning and logic. The figure was evil. Upon making the eye contact, I could feel his piercing red eyes staring into my bare soul, I felt the pain of a thousand volcanoes as if my body was being playfully thrust into the molten soup again and again. With great difficulty, I turned away from the demonic stare and just when I tried to come out of the bathroom, I slipped and fell.

---***---

I felt much better; I was lying on the bathroom with my face on the floor. The window in front of me was spewing sunshine generously, signaling to a new day. As I turned around, I saw a lot of commotion inside the bathroom. Several students as well as teachers had crowded around me.

'How did he die?' someone asked. 'Must be a heart…'

My smile ceased; I felt nothing. Nothing. Emptiness. Space. Vacuum. There lay my body, half outside the bathroom and half inside.

I felt the presence of someone beside me. I remembered him. The being from the previous night was there. He was not menacing nor deadly. He looked like a boy, a boy from our college perhaps?

'Ryan?' I asked him. He smiled and said nothing. He didn't have to say anything, for I understood that I was already a part of his world where words didn't matter.

We both looked ahead.

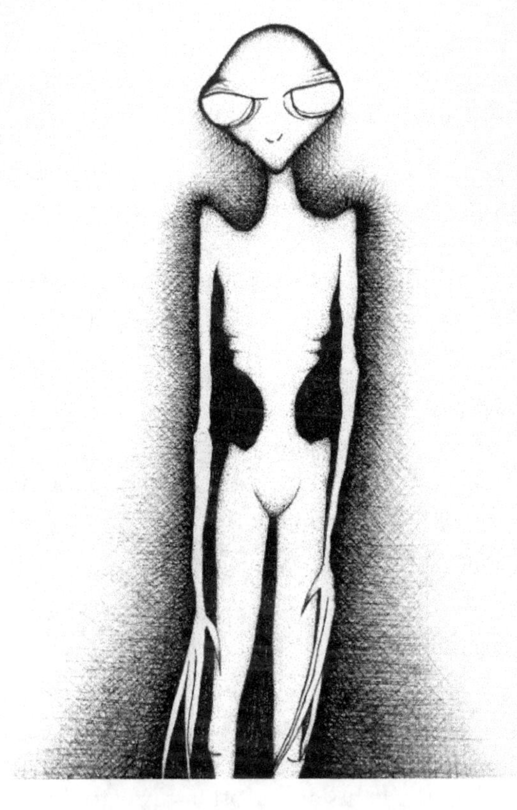

The lights, they say, have the power to kill

But not all of us are frightened still.

Unless the lights decide to harm the ones we love,

We don't feel the pain and stay inside the protected cove!

DEVIL'S IVY
~Desmond White~

'You applied to that library?' Mother says.

'I did,' I reply. 'Just waiting to hear back.'

I'm on the couch, looking at shapes on the ceiling. Mom is pruning. She takes the scissors, the ones on the desk and cuts the palm looming over the filing cabinet, the leaves that touch our face when we walk to the bathroom.

I've almost given up trying. Words are hard for me. When I was eleven, my speech slurred and doctors found a deflated basketball in my skull. (Obviously, I mean a tumor) Now I like to imagine there's a cave in there, lurking medusas and creatures made of echoes.

Like every millennial, I live at home, but I have better excuses. Seizures, nosebleeds, depression, they sound like a great heaving thing in my throat. Mother's apartment is a sanctuary from a world that ignores broken girls.

I've almost given up trying to tell her. But there are things important enough to bring back. There are things that do more damage in forgetting.

'Mother, there is no job at the library,' I say.

Mother looks outside. Maybe—? Then there's a flicker, like someone turned up the lights and Mother turns to the dracaena by the couch. The plant sits on a pedestal because it's not good for the cats. Dracaenas are my favorite—green hooks with lime wedges. The name means female dragon.

Snip, snip.

'Have you applied yet?' she asks.

'Not yet,' I reply, exhausted. The ceiling plaster looks like a face- amorphous and angry, scattered by wrinkles that make no sense. She doesn't remember the words I just said.

On the bookshelf, Mother waters the devil's ivy which hangs brown. It's called the devil's ivy because it's unkillable, but Mother's trying her best. I'm waiting for food. It comes around this time. Sits by the door. The Grub Hub delivery man forgets to knock.

I first noticed it in the streets. I saw a man sitting on the sidewalk. He raised his hands, shaking, to brood on brown fingers. The lights came. The man stood, no longer concerned. Then there was the woman in the bakery who cut her wrists. She was crying behind the counter. The lights came. She handed me an apple tart, eyes mid-lip, blood running on wax paper.

I thought I was crazy- a new symptom of half a brain. Then Mother told me about the lights. Not by saying anything, but by the words she abandoned.

We keep a money plant on the ledge above the kitchen sink because the cats don't go there. The leaves are toxic to cats, maybe people too. Mother was removing the dead, speaking of Brian, speaking of the time we went sledding on the hill by school, when the bulbs flickered.

When she stopped, I made a sound, prodding her to continue. I remember Brian. I always want to remember Brian. He had shaggy hair, the kind that girls like to touch with their hands. Not always kind, but resilient, with just the first traces of a mustache.

'Brian?' she said, putting yellow leaves in a plastic bag.

The lights had gone *snip, snip*. They'd tossed Brian into an ephemeral psychic wastebasket.

No matter how many pictures I showed her, Brian was a stranger. A friend of mine from school, maybe. Not the son she bore, the child who died painfully.

I had seen the lights but not here, in my home, breaking into Mother's skull and removing my brother like a tumor.

Then I knew.

The lights were pruning, ensuring people kept thinking in a way that's important to the lights.

But I am immune. There is something I am missing, something that would have made me vulnerable. And I'm sure it was once tucked in my mind, wrapped in corruption.

The windows flash. Brighter this time. 'What is it?' Mother asks, anxious of my steady concentration. 'Our neighbors?'

I see someone fall on their knees. Pain? I've never seen the lights cause pain before.

I have thought for a long time about the creatures behind the glow. Like every garden, there must be rules. They must be encouraging growths, clearing clutter, making incisions with tools sly enough to splice neurons without damage. Clipping memories, trimming hedges, correcting defects, removing disease.

Mother's shears have purpose. The plants, too. Some are for decoration. Some for eating. Mint, thyme, basil.

'Mother,' I say, 'the job at the library was years ago. Brian was the one who applied. He worked there before—before he died.'

Most of my speech is slurred but she is looking at me with confusion. There's suffering in her face. Something below the surface is trying to tunnel out. Then my eyes hurt at the glare. My hand burns. I see a red scar on my palm.

This is new. A warning. They can't have me, but they can take a swipe. I must be like a browning vine out of reach of the clippers. Or the spider who crawls between the roots.

'Mother,' I say. I don't know why I feel so desperate. 'You have a son named Brian. He died.'

Her face. Like a cat about to hiss.

Then the lights arrive. Bright. Brighter. Staying longer this time. I can tell they're hurting her. She sits at the table, palms against her forehead.

'Stop,' she groans.

'Mother—

'Stop,' she says louder.

Outside, silhouettes bend over. Whatever the light has been growing inside them, pulling, breaking—

The people have come to fruition.

Places that are quaint and beautiful are cold and the best.

They are quiet and calm until the thunder and the storm.

One such place was Robin's Nest-

A guest house that came to life when the spirits were ready to perform!

ROBIN'S NEST
~Enakshi J.~

The cold rush of the wind and the eerie silence added to the lonely surroundings. I was in Nainital with all my cousins. Yes, the elders were there too. It was a ritual we followed during the summer break. Spending our time in Nainital in Robin's Nest was something that we all looked forward to. Situated just 150 km away from Bareilly, this hill station provided the much-needed respite from the sweltering heat and the incessant sweating during the summer months. That year, too, we had gone to Robin's Nest unaware of the bizarre encounter that awaited us or rather me.

Robin's Nest was a palatial guest house and since it belonged to our family friends, we always had the whole house to ourselves. The main door had glass panels and an iron mesh for safety. It opened into a huge hall that had comfortable chairs placed in one corner and the other corner was occupied by a brown sofa set. The area in the centre had a gramophone that wouldn't work and that was topped by an abstract acrylic painting on the wall. There was something about that painting that made us all do a double-take when we first saw it. The blend of the blues and the shimmering silver in layers made it come to life. The hall was connected to the dining area and one of the bedrooms. The floral print on the wallpaper, lavish furniture beside the fireplace and translucent curtains added to the beauty of the first room. Upon asking the caretaker, we were told that the house belonged to a British ruler and was bought by an Indian, who, thereafter, passed it on to his children. The ground floor had three bedrooms. The second bedroom had the prayer area. Even though the wall of the prayer area was decorated with umpteen number of picture frames of Gods and Goddesses, the bearskin being used as a carpet could make anyone jump out of their skin! The third bedroom was every couple's dream. White flowy curtains, a king-size bed, a horizontal seating area beside the huge windows and a subtle wallpaper that evoked love and compassion- all these elements made that bedroom quite different from the rest of the rooms. The first floor was scarier, for no one really ever took over those bedrooms. The ground floor would always be enough for the ten of us to stay. The two bedrooms on the first floor were connected by a small passageway and there in the centre lay a brown chest. Our curiosity often forced us to open the chest but there would be some interruption or the other that would foil our plan.

That night the eerie silence had grown immensely. The only sounds that could be heard were the howling of the wind and the rustling of the leaves. The dark clouds made it nearly impossible to see the clear sky. It was pitch dark and so windy that when we went outside in the garden just to see if it had started raining, it seemed like even the wind was fearful of the unanticipated. A strong icy gust pushed us back indoors. With our parents shouting at us for letting the dust enter the house, we had no other option than to close the door and witness the thunderstorm through the rectangular glass panel. My aunt had asked the cook to leave early owing to the bad weather and we were on our own for dinner. I could hear the beating of the eggs in a glass bowl. I knew bread omelette was our only option. Just then, putting a halt to my racing thoughts, the youngest cousin asked, 'Shall we all play hide and seek?'

Everybody was thrilled but I wasn't. Being the eldest I couldn't admit that I was scared yet I could sense an uncanny feeling of void gripping my being.

'The eldest becomes the denner (seeker),' they all shouted unanimously.

'What? No! That's unfair,' I protested.

'Oh, come on Tina. Don't be fussy. It's just a game,' pushed my aunt.

'Yes, a game that might just scare me to death,' I wanted to say but preferred to keep the words to myself.

'Okay, what's the boundary?' I asked.

'Of course, the whole house!' They shouted unanimously again.

'No, not happening. Only two rooms,' I suggested.

'That's too less of an area. At least allow us to hide anywhere on the ground floor,' asked Veer, my brother.

I gave in because I knew they wouldn't budge. I was supposed to close my eyes and count till hundred and I did. When I opened my eyes to look around, I could see no one. That was obvious, wasn't it? I paced through the hallway towards the dining area where the large bulb that hung over the dining table swayed in monotony. The light was dim. I checked the kitchen and the adjacent storeroom but no one was there. I then headed to the room with the prayer area and spotted pink polka-dotted cloth peeking out. I was sure that Ria, one of my cousins, was hiding behind the bed. I tip-toed towards her and when I bent to catch her, the sight scared me out of my wits. She wasn't there. Only a piece of cloth that had the same design as her frock lay still on the floor. Running towards where the elders were supposed to be, I tripped twice on the carpet that wasn't there when I turned to crosscheck. I couldn't find anyone in the kitchen. There was no one in the dining room as well. I searched the storeroom, the bedrooms, the bathrooms, the hallway- still I couldn't find anyone. As I leaned on the wooden table to catch my breath, the sudden sound of people talking caught me off guard. The voice was faint. I walked towards the source only to find that it came from the first floor.

'Mona aunty, are you upstairs?' I screamed.

There was no response. Suddenly, I heard a man's voice too.

'Shobhit uncle, are you there? What are you all doing upstairs?'

Not receiving any response, I gathered all my courage and decided to check it out myself. Chanting in my mind that ghosts didn't exist, I climbed the wooden staircase. The creaking wood made me quake in my boots! I could still hear the voices. I was sure they all were upstairs.

'What is in here? Let's open this,' I heard Ria speak.

Wondering why she wasn't hiding, I called out to her but she didn't hear.

'It's locked. Where is the key?' I could hear Veer.

'Veer, are you all not playing anymore? Someone could have at least told me,' I said annoyed at how they all were up to something else.

Veer didn't respond nor did Ria. My parents, aunts, uncles-none of them responded. But I was sure that they all were upstairs. The passageway was empty. As I turned towards the bedroom on the right, my eyes spotted the open lid of the chest.

'Were they all trying to open this chest?' I wondered, 'But where did they go?'

I called out to them all again. The faint sound of a lullaby caught my attention. It came from the chest and it kept growing louder. It was like the chest was calling out to me. I was in a trance and didn't know what I was doing. The agenda of finding my family was no longer a priority. I was hypnotised by the sound. I wanted to see what lay inside the chest and so, I walked towards it. Placed right in the centre, the chest had glass windows around it. One could have a complete view of the garden from there.

While my subconscious told me to focus on the lullaby, my mother's words echoed in my logical side of the brain- 'Be aware. There is always a light that guides you through the dark walkway. Be aware.' She had told me that when I was not able to decide if I would survive alone in the college hostel. She had often told me that, if at any point, I find myself between the devil and the deep blue sea, I should look out for the light. It would just be there- still and persistent- ready to guide me. The bizarre sensations in my body had increased. As I went closer to the chest, the goose bumps became visible. And just then, when I was about to take a look inside the chest, the glimmering light outside the window caught my attention. I tried to look outside and found all of them. My entire family was out there in the garden! The light came from my uncle's mobile phone who tried to focus it on me, mumbling something that I couldn't hear. Then it struck me. That was the light!

I rushed downstairs to tell them all about what I had heard and seen.

'Where were you, Tina?' asked my mother.

'We all called you so many times but you didn't answer. We thought you were in the washroom,' said Ria.

'I was right there in the hallway but I didn't find any of you,' I faltered.

'How is it possible? We came outside just moments back when we heard a sudden thud. We thought the Banyan had fallen!' My uncle spoke as he tried to calm me down.

'I thought you all were upstairs.'

'How can that happen? We decided, remember, that none of us would go upstairs,' asked Veer as he passed his hand over his forehead and looked puzzled.

'But I heard your voices. You all were speaking about the chest and the key that could open the lock, weren't you?' I queried.

'No, we weren't, dear. Come here. Let me check if you have temperature,' said my aunt and touched my forehead with her cold hand.

'All's well here. You must be just dreaming then, I guess,' spoke another one of my cousins.

'Mother, I am not lying. I heard the voices so I ran upstairs to check if you all are there. When I reached there, I saw the chest open and I heard a sweet lullaby…'

'What? Did you say that you went upstairs?' asked my aunt.

'Yes, because I thought you all were there. I also saw a piece of pink polka-dotted cloth behind the bed. I thought Ria was hiding there but it was just the cloth. I think Ria would have torn her dress,' I gestured towards Ria who was busy inspecting her dress.

'My dress is not torn, didi,' she confirmed.

Somewhere in the back of my mind, I knew what was happening. I wasn't hallucinating. Something paranormal had just happened inside the house. I was worried more because I was the chosen one and that scared the living daylights out of me. My mother consoled me and we all went inside. The Banyan had not fallen. We couldn't figure out the reason behind the loud thud. Maybe it happened so that I could be saved from the unforeseen event. Or maybe it was just a coincidence- a coincidence that saved my life. My aunts, uncles, cousins and my brother didn't believe me but my mother's expression gave me a feeling of reassurance. I knew that she knew. That was enough. That night, I couldn't sleep, for sleep would open another door to make things worse. I just hugged my mother and pretended to be in a deep slumber. In the middle of the night, I heard the same lullaby again and when I tried to focus a little, I could make out that it came from the bathroom in our room. I didn't move nor did I open my eyes even once. I just prayed. I just prayed that we all survive the night.

The cryptic encounter with the unknown left me fearful. Fortunately, we were supposed to leave the next day and that came as a relief. Such things didn't occur again. Maybe something was there in Robin's Nest that came to life that fateful night. I was glad that I could make it out sane and alive. As destiny would have it, we couldn't go to that place again after that owing to time constraints and the fact that now two of us were in college and the others had their board exams. I think growing up actually saved me from another harrowing experience. Now even when my cousins talk about planning a visit to Robin's Nest, I am always the first one to make up an excuse and spoil the plan.

The cemented walls and the emptiness-

House an evil spirit that yearns to be let out,

If only people realized how it is to be trapped within the nothingness,

They would give in to the pleas without a doubt!

FLAT NO. 413
~Gunjan Rathore~

'Yes, yes, keep this bag here, thank you,' Yamini opened the purse, took out the money and gave it to the taxi driver. Rishi and Yamini had their first day in the flat. 'Finally, we have found the flat like we always wanted, but this flat is very expensive for us.' Rishi said to Yamini.

'Now the expenses are only going to increase as after some months, our baby will also arrive in this world. I am so excited, Rishi,' chirped Yamini. Rishi kissed her gently on her forehead.

'I am excited too; I can't wait for the day when our child will be born and our family will be complete. But it's too late now. The baby and the mother need to sleep,' announced Rishi.

'Okay, Daddy.' Looking at Yamini's face made Rishi smile. They were happy.

'Yes, mummy, we have arrived at our new house. No, we haven't performed the *Pooja* yet. It is late. We will do it tomorrow morning, Ma. In fact, I think your God will be fast asleep at this hour and he will not like to be disturbed,' persuaded Rishi.

'But it is important that you...' He cut his mother short by changing the topic entirely. 'You take care, now. We will call you in the morning, okay?' he ended the conversation with a rhetorical question and hung up.

'Isn't Mummy asking about performing *Pooja*?' asked Yamini and continued, 'Even I was thinking of this, Rishi. It doesn't feel right. We have come straight into a new house, we haven't opened the boxes yet, the idols are still packed and we haven't performed the *Pooja* as well. I think we should...' Yamini was interrupted by Rishi.

'Dear, it is 11:00 p.m. It is quite late and I am really very tired after all the packing and then moving. Can we sleep now, please? I promise that the first thing we will do in the morning is unpack our things,' he requested.

Even Yamini was tired after the day's work. She agreed with her husband and both of them called it a day. Praying to the idols could wait, couldn't it?

'Good night,' said Rishi and was immediately taken aback when he saw the bottle of sleeping pills in his wife's hand.

'What is this? I have told you so many times not to take these pills anymore. You are pregnant and these are harmful not only for the baby but also for you. I know you have been taking these pills for a long time but you need to understand the risks now.'

'But Rishi, I am not able to sleep without these. Moreover, these have been prescribed by the doctor as well. She said that I can take them twice a week, so what's the harm?'

'Okay, if that's the case, we will go to the doctor tomorrow itself and check with her if these pills can be substituted by something natural- something that doesn't have side effects. Now, let's sleep, my love!' Rishi put his arm around Yamini and they both closed their eyes.

---***---

'Yamini, wake up,' Rishi shouted, 'wake up, Yami…' His voice trailed off. His quivering voice was scary.

"What happened? It is 2:00 in the morning. Are you alright?' said Yamini squinting at the wall clock.

'Yamini,' screamed Rishi again, 'I want you to wake up. Why wouldn't you wake up?'

Rubbing her eyes, Yamini tried to open them and then gasped because no one was there before her.

'Rishi, where are you?' queried Yamini, 'Please don't play pranks at this hour. At least let me sleep peacefully for some more time. Now, come on, tell me where you are,' she chided no one in particular.

Not getting any response, she switched on the light only to find that the light wouldn't turn on. 'What happened? Is there a power cut? Rishi, where are you?'

It became difficult for her to bear any more and thus she called out to her husband again, 'Where are you? I am scared now.'

Pacing across the room with resolute footsteps, she searched for him and when she couldn't find him, she grabbed the torch and went out of the room to look for him. The sudden movement of the curtains caught her off guard. Upon checking, she realized that the doors and the windows were all shut. A chill ran down her spine.

'I cannot believe that you want to do this now! Where are you, Rishi? I am going to speak to Mummy tomorrow and tell her about all this nonsense. It's enough now. Tell me where you are. And why is the power not there?' she finished in one breath.

Feeling someone's breath on her neck, she turned around only to find no one there. She tried to run away from there but the invisible clutches seemed quite strong. They held her back while she moaned in pain. Tears rolled down her eyes as she couldn't think of what she could do to avert the misery.

'Yamini, I will kill you. How much will you run from me?' came a voice so harsh that it shocked Yamini more.

'Kill me? Who are you and why do you want to kill me? Please show yourself. Where is my husband? Rishi, is this you?' Yamini shot an array of questions. She sat on the floor, tired. 'Where is my husband?' she murmured, 'What have you done to him? Please tell me,' she pleaded.

The sudden movement in the dark alerted her and she got up with a jerk. Rushing towards the silhouette, she asked, 'Rishi, where are you running? What is happening?'

'Yamini, I am here only. What happened? Tell me. Why are you crying? What happened?'

'Rishi, all these voices…'

'Which voices?'

'Didn't you hear them?'

'No, not at all.'

'But there was someone- more like a shadow. He said to me that he would kill me and…'

'Somebody wanted to kill you, but why?''

'I don't know, Rishi. I don't know anything. I just feel something is not right in this house. From the moment we have entered, things have been happening. I think there is a presence in this house besides us.'

'But the doors are shut?'

'No, Rishi, I mean to say that this house is haunted.'

'Haunted?' Rishi laughed, 'Darling, do you believe in all these things? Come on, there is no one here, trust me.'

'We didn't perform *Pooja*. I think it is happening because of that.'

'Yamini, it is just in your mind. You are assuming things that do not exist. Just because we didn't do *Pooja* doesn't mean that this house is haunted.'

'I am not assuming things. I heard him clearly, he wanted to…'

'…to kill you, didn't he?' asked Rishi, mocking his wife.

'Yes,' Yamini sobbed.

'So, let him kill you and your baby,' demanded Rishi.

Shocked by what he had said, Yamini was confused.

'What are you saying? I don't understand this. Why are you behaving so strangely?'

Rishi held her tight and laughed. 'I will kill you, Yamini, and I will do it right now.'

'Stop it. What's wrong with you? Stop pressing my arms and my belly. Something will happen to our child.'

'I will kill the baby too. Then you and the baby- both- can go to God and pray to him,' deadpanned Rishi.

'What nonsense? You are not Rishi! Who are you? Rishi, have you been possessed? Oh God, help us, please.'

Rishi loosened his grip on her when she pushed him towards the wall. His head hit the wall. Grabbing the opportunity, she ran towards the room, picking up her mobile phone on the way. Rishi chased her all the way and once inside the room, he snatched her phone and grinned from ear to ear.

'Help! Please, somebody help me.'

'Shout as much as you like. Nobody can hear you; nobody can help you. This night, I am going to put an end to all your misery.'

'No, Rishi. I beg you. Please don't hurt me. What wrong have I done?'

'Who is Rishi? He is not here. I am not him. And he is not coming anytime soon to save you!'

'Whoever you are, please be kind to me. I am pregnant, please don't kill me. I...I will leave this flat, but please leave me, please.' Yamini cried.

His eyes turned fierce red; he was ready to kill his wife. He took the knife out of his pocket and pulled Yamini by her waist. The tension on Yamini's face was evident in the form of the several wrinkles. Her eyes were swollen and tears wouldn't stop pouring out. She screamed loudly and that broke her reverie. It had all been a dream.

'What happened, Yamini?' asked Rishi who had been woken up by the shrill sound.

She did not answer. She seemed to be in a trance.

'Are you feeling cold? Should I increase the temperature of the AC?'

'AC...what?'

Yamini looked around. Rishi was in front of her. She was lying on the bed.

'What? Come on, say something. Why are you screaming at this time? Did you have a bad dream?'

'What nightmare? You were right there by the door, holding me close and about to...' her voice trailed off.

'I wasn't there. I was sleeping. Oh, I understand now. It is the side effect of these pills. I told you not to take those pills. See, what they are doing to you!'

'It is not the pills and I wasn't dreaming.'

Offering her a glass of water, Rishi soothed her by patting her back. However, Yamini was lost in different thoughts. She knew it wasn't a dream, for it felt so real. Something was wrong and she was upset because she didn't know what was.

'Maybe the exhaustion is taking a toll on you. After all, we did have a tough day, didn't we? Packing and then travelling- that's is too much already. Don't worry, everything is fine now. You need to go back to sleep so that you get ample rest.'

'This flat, Rishi. There is something ominous about this flat. We need to leave it,' she urged him.

'That's ridiculous. Just because you had a bad dream doesn't mean that there is something wrong with the house. You need to rest your eyes now. Come on, let's sleep.'

He said this and grinned again, the evil visible on his face. He was not himself and Yamini knew it. The only thing she didn't know was what she would do next. Just then, he whispered in her ear, 'Good night, Yamini. And just so you know, we aren't leaving this house at any cost. I like it here. It feels home. It feels as if I have been living here for a long time. Anyway, it is time to sleep now.' He laughed and the fierce redness was back in his eyes.

It reoccurs every other night in my dream.

I try as much to shun it out,

I try as much to blame it on my mind's occasional bout,

But it is there mocking, waiting for me to scream.

THE APPARITION
~Kumar Vikrant~

It wasn't dark yet; the fog was engulfing the city streets slowly. I was running madly in the deserted streets and that entity was chasing me. I felt my pace was slowing down and the distance between me and that entity was decreasing gradually. I was under a strange spell and the entity flew and took me in its embrace. I yelled in pain but no voice came out of my mouth; I was just breathless and trembling. Soon it was dark everywhere. This nightmare ended leaving me drenched in my sweat. My chest was still aching, I took a deep breath and thanked God for bringing me out of that nightmare.

Ten years later

Landing a government officer's job just after graduation was a dream come true but the training for that job called me 1230 km away from my home town in the far east. The hostel of the training institute was beside the deserted railway station of that city. The hostel was like a graveyard and the room allotted to me was number 13. I knew nothing about that number but as a latecomer, I had no other option but to accept that room. Most of the trainees who came for the three-month-long training programme got the best available rooms of that hostel. I, along with five other trainees, had to take Room no. 13 reluctantly. Soon we came to know about the notoriety of that room; the mess' staff told us that the room was haunted as three trainees had taken their lives by hanging themselves in that room years ago.

It was the stupidest thing we had heard but within a fortnight, we started having meaningless disputes amongst ourselves. All of us pondered over the matter and decided to get rid of that room at the earliest. Soon we found our chance as the previous batch of trainees left the hostel. Fortunate that we were, we occupied one of those vacant rooms.

Things became better and we began enjoying the training and hostel life. However, a long weekend changed it all for me. Since it was festival time, most of the trainees left for their homes. I, being so far away from my hometown, had to stay in the hostel. There was no way to go to my home and come back just within five days. Some of my roommates invited me to their homes but being an introvert, I refused their invitation politely.

The hostel was almost empty; there was hardly anyone left. Those who stayed back were either in a different wing or on a different floor. I used to meet them all at the time of breakfast, lunch and dinner. Two days passed and I became used to the solitary life of the hostel. On the third day, I napped a little after having my lunch. During that nap, someone knocked at my door. I got up and unlatched door but there was no one there. When I strained my neck to have a look at the corridor, I saw a thin boy clad in a vest and *lungi* (loincloth) going towards the washroom of that wing. It was strange because that attire was not permitted in the hostel premises. I felt an urge to see that boy and went behind him to the washroom. To my surprise, I could see no one in the washroom. I snapped my head because I thought that I was imagining things. Still, the sight of the boy sent jitters in my body.

I came back to my room but I couldn't push the sight of the thin boy out of my mind. In the evening, I went to the mess and had my dinner silently. I went to my bed early after switching off all the lights in my room. It was a moonlit night and my room was also a bit illuminated by the white light. My mind refused to give up on the thoughts of that boy. But soon sleep took over the reins and I fell asleep. I had no idea for how long I had slept but a strange convulsion woke me up. Even though my eyes were wide open, my body couldn't move. After a few minutes, I overcame that strange situation and looked around. The three beds in front of me were occupied by three shadows; they were sitting silently. The presence of those shadows terrified me and I was afraid to think that there was some connection between the momentary paralysation of my body and those shadows.

Fearful of those shadows, I got up and ran towards the door, unlatched it and ran barefooted towards the mess. Dark and scary, the buildings looked like tall towers that were ready to attack. Not being able to see any light inside the mess, I changed my mind and ran towards the main gate. The gate was locked and it would have been a wrong decision to wake up the security guard. Thankfully, it was not that high and that made it easier for me to jump on the other side. The railway station was not far away. Hence, I ran towards the station. I didn't look back even though the sharp pebbles hurt my bare feet. There were not many passengers at the railway station as it was 03:35 a.m. in the night. My trembling made me the centre of attention but I ignored all those who kept staring at me in amazement. All the benches were occupied by passengers who were sleeping peacefully. I just sat on the cold floor of the railway station and tried to control my feelings. Whatever I saw and went through couldn't be explained to anyone. I waited at the station till 08:00 a.m. and after that decided to head to the hostel mess. The mess staff was surprised to see me as I was late than usual. I told them everything and requested them to help me collect my belongings from the room. They complied. After the previous night's horror, no power in the world could force me to stay in that room.

Cold Muzzle

After the training, I was posted in a small town in North India. Living in the outskirts of that small town wasn't a big deal for me as I was from a small city and the serenity of the wilderness was rather soothing for me. A big house was my living place. That house was provided by the government. A peon from my office was looking after all my needs out there. I made him lock most of the rooms of that big house and kept only two of the rooms open for me- one for the guests and the other to be used as my bedroom.

It was alright but soon the serenity of that place was replaced by the invisible chaos that started in my bedroom. The uncanny sound in my bedroom disturbed me a lot. Soon, I got the news that I had qualified for a better job and I started looking forward to getting rid of that strange place.

During those days of dilemma, my sleep was infrequent. On one such restless night, I got up in the middle of the night. The darkness compelled me to stay in bed. I could feel the cold muzzle press hard against my chest. Something caught my attention. The stirring in the air engulfed my body. First, I thought that I was imagining things but then ended up screaming, 'Go away… go away!'

I jumped out of the bed and darted to switch on the light but there was no electricity. Left with no other option, I came out of that big house and sat under the street light. A little later, the peon came. I told him everything. Without giving any explanation, he just advised me to vacate that house immediately.

Nidhi... Nidhi, Come Outside...

I left that job, joined another and got married after a few years. As I was posted at UP-Uttarakhand border subdivision, I decided to live in a nearby Uttarakhand subdivision for some personal reasons. My wife, who was pregnant at that time, also lived with me. The rental house we were living in was part of a big house. We were living on the first floor; the landlady and her family were on the ground floor. It so happened that my wife, who had been facing several problems like restlessness and headache for a few days, told me to talk to her at night as that would make her feel better. It was not a big issue and we started talking for long hours till my wife felt a little better. One such night, at around 02:15 a.m., when we were busy talking to each other, we heard our landlady shouting my wife's name.

'Nidhi…Nidhi, come outside,' she screamed.

Her strange voice and an even stranger message disturbed us.

'Nidhi…Nidhi, come outside.'

This time the voice was clearer and closer.

My wife got up and went towards the door.

It was annoying; I said in anger, 'What are you doing?'

'Amma Ji is calling me,' said my wife, confusion evident on her face.

'No, you are not going out at this hour. Come back,' I ordered.

She came back and I called up the landlady. She picked the phone after several rings and said that she was not the one calling out to my wife, for she had been sleeping.

I told her whatever my wife and I had heard. Being generous and motherly, my landlady came upstairs to spend some time with my wife while I called up my mother to inform her about that incident. My mother panicked and asked us to return to our hometown as soon as possible.

Next day, the landlady told us that the vulnerable condition of a pregnant lady sometimes attracts bad spirits. It was impossible to go back or change that house immediately. But that generous landlady did her best to avert the negative energy by asking the priests to perform *Poojas* and getting the holy water sprayed in every corner.

Satanic Grip

Last winter, my brother-in-law's marriage got fixed. My wife and my daughter stayed with my in-laws as they, too, lived in my hometown. Since I could not afford to take so many leaves, I stayed back in our house in Uttrakhand. I would finish my work and return to my house in the evening. Lying on the bed, one night, I was chatting with my friends and I didn't realize that time flew past like a flip second. At 02:30 a.m., we all decided to wind up for the night and go to sleep.

I don't remember when I fell asleep but I do remember that the sleep was not a sound one. There were dreams, illogical dreams and finally, that entity reappeared after several decades. That time, it simply cornered me in a deserted street, it wrapped its furry arms around me and I screamed in pain. No voice came out of my throat. I gasped for breath and I woke up. It was a nightmare but my chest, around which that entity wrapped its arms, was still aching. The pain was unbearable.

All the memories came rushing back. I couldn't sleep, for I could not understand the connection among those cryptic encounters. It all began in the hostel and then continued to the village in North India. If that was not enough, it continued to haunt me there in the new house as well. Since I was the only witness, I do not know if I was hallucinating! I could be. But then when I think of the strange voice that called out to my wife the other night, it scares the daylights out of me. Both of us had heard it, so it cannot be a mere dream. Something terrible did happen that night. We still feel uneasy whenever we both think about that night. *What if my wife had gone outside following the instructions of that voice?*

All these incidents force me to think if these entities have limited powers just to terrify someone? Or are they just the creation of a chemical *imbalance* in my brain?

But that strange voice which my wife and I heard couldn't be a prank, could it? I still wonder why couldn't the power behind that voice enter in our bedroom?

It is also true that despite not having a logical explanation of those events, I'm not ready to accept the reality of ghosts and apparitions.

I roam about in the darkness of the night,

There are some fears and guilt that I like to fight.

I wait for the spirits to come to that place,

For I would like to plead guilty face-to-face.

THE CHRISTENSEN BROTHERS
(A Play)
~Michael J Moore~

CHARACTERS

Marshal: 17 years old.
Alan: 13 years old.
Ray: Scruffy man in his early to mid-forties.

SETTING

Marshal and Alan in a car, driving through farmland (in rural America) at night.

"/" indicates overlapping lines.

Marshal is driving. Alan is in the passenger seat.

MARSHAL: You tired?

ALAN: I've been tired.

MARSHAL: *Yawns.*
Yeah. It's been a long day, hasn't it?

ALAN: Well, technically the day's over.

MARSHAL: Okay. Long night then.

ALAN: No longer than any other night.

MARSHAL: I get that, genius. It just feels like we've been driving forever now. You ever think it might be a miracle you met Tina?

ALAN: No. It was the exact opposite of a miracle. We went to school together, we met in sixth period, Math. It was actually quite organic.

MARSHAL: Whoa buddy! Keep that stuff to yourself. You wanna make me sick?

Beat.

MARSHAL: I'm not saying it's a miracle there're girls at your school. Most middle-schools got 'em. Too bad I'm gonna graduate before you make it to high school though. I could've showed you how to really drive 'em crazy.

ALAN: Do you have a point, Marshal?

MARSHAL: Of course, I do. What was I saying again?

ALAN: I don't think anyone, but you know most of the time.

MARSHAL: Right! The miracle! All I'm saying is—how many countries do you think there are in the world—give or take?

ALAN: How am I supposed to know?

MARSHAL: I dunno. You're the smart one. Fine. The world's big, right? And out of everywhere Tina could've been born and gone to school, she ended up in the same place, at the same time as you. Think about it, man. The only girl in history who ever could've put up with you. What are the chances?

ALAN: I take it you're referring to my condition.

MARSHAL: You see?

ALAN: See what?

MARSHAL: That's what I mean, right there. I don't know if I'm supposed to answer, or you'll just tell me that you didn't even ask a question.

ALAN: I didn't.

MARSHAL: *In a game-show announcer's voice.*
And there it is!

Beat.

MARSHAL: You take everything too literal, man. And you have a hundred and forty IQ. That's not a condition, it's a gift.

ALAN: How do you know my IQ?

MARSHAL: You're my baby brother, Alan. I used to change your diapers. I know a lot more than just your IQ, if ya know what I'm saying—

ALAN: Hey! What did Mom tell you when she said we could borrow the car? No teasing me!

MARSHAL: I'm not. I mean—I dunno. Maybe I am, just a little. Lighten up, man. I'm just saying maybe you milk this Asperger's thing a bit.

ALAN: Can we change the subject?

MARSHAL: Your call, buddy. You tired?

ALAN: I've been tired.

MARSHAL: *Yawns.*
Yeah. You're telling me. It's been a long day. How long have we been on the road now?

ALAN: *Shrugs.*

MARSHAL: Man, I'm gonna have to get back into shape if I'm gonna make the football team next year. I don't know if it was swimming in the lake all day, or the sun, but I'm beat.

ALAN: When are you not beat, Marshal?

MARSHAL: Was that a joke? Nice! See? You can lighten up when you want to.

ALAN: Okay. Okay. Let's not make a big thing out of it.

MARSHAL: Man, it's so dark out here. Streetlights would be nice, don't you think?

ALAN: This highway's all farmland. No streetlights out here.

MARSHAL: I noticed. I always thought it was kinda creepy driving out here at night though. Nothing but trees, fields, and cows. Is it just me, or are cows kinda creepy?

ALAN: Just you.

MARSHAL: Come on, man. I mean—-

Plugs his nose and makes a cow noise, then looks at his brother expectantly.

ALAN: *Shakes his head.*

MARSHAL: Naw?

ALAN: No.

MARSHAL: Hm. Weird.

ALAN: *Takes a deep breath, blows a raspberry.*

MARSHAL: You know, I'm glad you didn't bring Tina today.

ALAN: You're just jealous because you don't have a girlfriend.

MARSHAL: Really? We're gonna go there?

ALAN: Hey, I'm just saying—

MARSHAL: I'm just saying. I've had twice as many girlfriends as years you've been alive, little guy. You know what though? I'm proud of you. She's cool too. But when's the last time you and I got to hang out together?

ALAN: Well, there was—

MARSHAL: Don't answer. It was rhetorical. I'm just saying I had a good time today. We should do it again before the summer's out, don't you think?

ALAN: Sure. Maybe next time you won't be afraid to swim out to the deep part of the Lake.

MARSHAL: What? Another joke? Okay. I'll take it. And maybe next time you won't run away from a duck.

ALAN: Hey! That thing could have had rabies!

Ray appears kneeling by the highway, looking down at two wooden crosses.

MARSHAL: *Looks at his brother and smiles.*
Yeah?

ALAN: Yeah.

MARSHAL: *Looks back at the road.*
Okay. You tired?

ALAN: I've been tired.

MARSHAL: *Yawns.*
Yeah, it's been a long—whoa! What the hell?

ALAN: What?

MARSHAL: *Leans forward. Squints out the windshield.*
You see that?

ALAN: See what?

MARSHAL: Right there. Is that a person?

ALAN: What? Where?

MARSHAL: Right there. By the road.
Turns the steering wheel.

ALAN: What are you doing?

MARSHAL: I'm pulling over. There's someone there. Just wait here, okay?

ALAN: Marshal! No! Just keep driving!

But Marshal steps out, shivers, and rubs his exposed forearms as he approaches Ray from behind. Alan climbs out and steps up next to his brother.

MARSHAL: Hey! Excuse me? Sir? Are you okay?

RAY: *Not looking back. His voice is slightly slurred.*
I'm fine. Please go away.

MARSHAL: You can't just sit out here, man. It's dark. Someone's gonna run you over.

RAY: I said I'm fine! Just leave me alone.

MARSHAL: Look, I'm not supposed to give anyone a ride, but if you need me to call someone, I can. You live nearby?

RAY: Right here.

MARSHAL: You live right here?

RAY: Of course, I don't live right here! Do you see any houses? Right here is where it happened. There used to be a tree. A big one. They cut it down after the accident.

MARSHAL: You had an accident here?

ALAN: *Grabs his brother's arm.*
Let's get outta here.

MARSHAL: *Pulls away.*
No. We can't just leave this guy in the middle of nowhere.

RAY: Yes, you can, son. And you should. I'm a bad man.

MARSHAL: You been drinking or something?

RAY: Yes.

MARSHAL: We're gonna get you some help, okay? Why don't you come and wait by the car?

ALAN: No. Don't bring him back to the car.

MARSHAL: *Glares at his brother, disgusted.*
What? What's wrong with you?

ALAN: You know you're not supposed to let anyone in Mom's car. Can we please just go?

MARSHAL: I didn't say anything about him getting inside. We can't leave him like this though. He's drunk and cars can't see when they come around this corner. He could get hit.

RAY: I'd deserve it. I'd deserve whatever happened to me.

MARSHAL: You're talking crazy, man. Come on, lemme get you—

RAY: I killed 'em. Right here. This is where I did it. You know I haven't had a drink since that night? Not till now, at least. I been back here a few times, but I try and avoid it. I'd rather drive five miles outta the way. Isn't that crazy?

MARSHAL: Whoa. Back up a second. You killed someone?

RAY: More than one someone?

ALAN: Please! Can we just go? We have to get home or Mom's gonna be mad!

RAY: I suppose you're here to see 'em, ain't you

MARSHAL: See who?

RAY: You know who! Tonight's the night they say they show up. Once a year on the anniversary of their death. The ghosts. *Makes apparition hand gesture.*

Whoooooooo! You know, the first couple years I didn't make it 'cause I was serving my time. Yeah, I only did two years.

Apparently driving drunk and killing folks ain't a big deal in this state. Then, when I got out, I still didn't come. I couldn't bring myself to do it.

ALAN: I don't like this!
Covers his ears.

I'm getting back in the car! You need to come with!
Walks back to the passenger side and takes a seat, where he watches intently.

RAY: Stupid small-town kids ain't got nothing better to do than start rumours about dead people. Well, sorry to crash your party, kid, but there ain't gonna be no ghosts here tonight. Just the drunk who ghosted 'em. If you're smart, that'd scare you even more.

MARSHAL: Listen man, it sounds like it was an accident.

RAY: Accident? Is that what it sounds like to you? You know why I came here tonight? Seven years later? Do you know why I got piss-drunk and walked hours out into the middle of nowhere? Because I can't live with this guilt anymore! I came here to off myself!

MARSHAL: To kill yourself?

RAY: To kill myself! I didn't bring a gun though. No sleeping pills. I had this crazy idea that I'd wait till a car came around that corner, and I would just throw myself under it. You hearing me? I was gonna cause another accident. Kill a few more innocents. Why not? I can't do any worse than I already did, can I? Turns out I'm not just a murderer though. I'm a coward too. Couldn't bring myself to do it.

MARSHAL: What's your name, man?

RAY: What does it matter? I'm cursed! Is that your brother in that car back there?

MARSHAL: *Glances back at Alan.*
Yeah.

RAY: What if it would've been you and him I hit?

MARSHAL: I mean—I don't—

RAY: How old are you anyway, kid?

MARSHAL: I'm seventeen.

RAY: One a the boys I killed was your age. Other was thirteen.

ALAN: *Steps out of the car.*

RAY: They were brothers. One of 'em was disabled. Still sound like an innocent accident to you? Just two babies driving back from a day at the lake, and I—I—God—
Puts his face in his hands and sobs as Alan walks up and stands next to his brother.
—Oh God.

ALAN: Marshal please. Can we just go? I'm scared.

MARSHAL: Alan, I think we know this guy.

Ray falls still and just sniffs.

ALAN: I know.

RAY: *Through tears.*
No.

ALAN: Marshal.

RAY: No! No! / No! No!

MARSHAL: I'm scared too, Alan.

RAY: *Stands up and turns to face them. Both boys gasp and stare in frozen horror as he speaks.*

This can't be real. You're not real. There's no such thing as—
but you're-Marshal?
Takes a step toward them. They step back.
Alan?
Takes another step. They once again step back.

The rumours—They're—I'm sorry. I'm so sorry. I didn't
mean to kill you. The corner was too sharp and that tree
shouldn't of—I never meant to—
Reaches out to touch Marshal.

MARSHAL: *Jerking away and yelling.*
You're a liar!

RAY: Now you're dead. You're both dead and I walked away
with hardly a / scratch—

MARSHAL: Alan, get back in the car! Don't listen to him!

ALAN: Come with me. Please Marshal.
Both boys run and jump in the car.

MARSHAL: I am!

RAY: No! Don't go! / Lemme make it right! Please! You're
lost. You can't just keep driving forever!

MARSHAL: Shut your door! Quick!

*Both boys shut their doors and Ray's voice is cut off. He disappears
again as they drive past him. The brothers breathe heavily and don't
speak at first. Then, finally, Marshal smiles.*

MARSHAL: You tired?

ALAN: I've been tired.

MARSHAL: *Yawns.*
Yeah. Me too. It's been a long day.

ALAN: That's impossible.

MARSHAL: It's a figure of speech, Alan.

ALAN: I know.

MARSHAL: *Looks at his brother lovingly, and shakes his head.* Doesn't it feel like we've been driving a long time?

ALAN: Yeah.

MARSHAL: Like we should be home by now?

ALAN: Just keep driving, Marshal.

MARSHAL: I had a good time today. I'm glad you didn't bring Tina.

ALAN: Yeah.

x-x-x

PS: This story has not been edited by the editor. The dialect used is in accordance with the author's choice.

They call me brave as they think I am unafraid.

They call me bold as I never hide behind anyone's shade.

What they don't know is that fear is my middle name,

For the spirits and the ghosts, often, do not sound so lame!

SUMERPUR JUNCTION
~Samrat Sahu~

Being in a city like Bangalore was always fascinating for me until I heard and visited Sumerpur which was my hometown; the town where my grandparents lived. Like every other typical story, mine was also the same- Grandparents were residing in the village, father had come to Bangalore for a job and had settled here. We had been living in Bangalore for 27 years and that was a long time.

'Mahir, we are going to our village to celebrate your grandparents' 50th anniversary,' my father said in an exciting tone.

'But father, I have never been to that place. What would I do over there?' I queried.

'I know and that is why I am taking you there so that you can see our house and our farms. This way you can meet your grandparents as well. They miss you so much!' My father tried to sound convincing.

'But father, we can call them here and celebrate it grandly. Why do we need to go to the village?' I tried to argue.

'Yes, of course, we can but your grandfather insists on seeing you and your little sister this time. He wants you to meet others in the village, socialize with them a little and feel connected to the place.' Knowing that my father wouldn't surrender that easily, I gave up and didn't argue the toss. The plan was finalized and we were set to go to Sumerpur.

I hadn't talked to my mother about the trip at all and thus, I figured out that she might be my only chance of escaping the plan. Hence, I tried to ask her if the plan could be cancelled. To my surprise, she admitted that even she didn't want to go. The reason behind her disinterest shocked me even more.

'Sumerpur is not a normal place; it is cursed. This village is located in the Eastern UP and comprises of 700-800 people only. It is a hive of abnormal activity. Some say that the curse comes alive at night while some say that spirits reside in that village.'

The mere idea of a haunted place made me giggle. Contrary to my mother's expectation, I was interested in visiting that place, for I believed that the supernatural beings only existed in one's imagination. They did not exist in reality.

I still remember 18th March, the day we boarded our flight from Bangalore to reach Lucknow. From there, we had to travel in a passenger train to reach the village. That was the thing about villages- they lacked connectivity. We reached Sumerpur at around 8:00 p.m. Quiet and creepy, the place had limited number of shops around the station. There were two small rooms designated as ticket counter and Station Master, respectively. The typical yellow board on the wall caught my attention; it read 'Sumerpur Junction'.

I don't know if people would believe me or not but the moment I stepped down from the railway coach, I sensed something negative in the ambience. Surrounded by darkness, I couldn't see any living being in the vicinity. Other than the flickering street light and the bowing tress, no one cared to welcome us. The wind was warm and it made the leaves rustle now and then. The whistling sound was perfect for the music.

It just took us ten minutes to walk to our house. Everybody was waiting there. I met my grandparents, had dinner and went to sleep, for there was nothing much to do. Due to lack of connectivity, I couldn't operate my phone much. I had to share my bed with Nikhil, my uncle's elder son. To initiate a small talk, I asked Nikhil if the rumours about that place were true.

'Nikhil, do you believe that there are spirits in this village?' I asked.

'I don't know much but yes, there are certain places where people say that they have witnessed something and felt something paranormal,' Nikhil replied.

'Can we go to all those places?' I queried, my tone reeking of excitement rather than fear.

'Of course, why not! You are here for a few days after all. I will show you around those places but remember not to tell this to anyone or else they wouldn't allow us to venture out.'

He was right and hence, we decided not to let the cat out of the bag at any cost.

Beginning our day normally the next day, Nikhil and I finished the chores quickly as we had different plans. While others were busy, we decided to slip out when nobody was noticing.

'Mahir, listen,' Nikhil called out.

'Yes, Nikhil, what happened?'

'Since you seemed so excited about the paranormal stuff, I thought of surprising you. I asked my friend, Keyur, to send me the videos of the paranormal sightings. Here you go. I hope you like them. But don't get scared,' Nikhil grinned from ear to ear.

'What kind of videos?' I asked.

'These are the videos of the bank and the government school. People spotted something uncanny. See for yourself,' he passed the phone to me.

In the first video, I could see a lot of people talking, eating and enjoying. Probably they constituted the bank staff. There seemed nothing wrong in the video and just when I was about to fast-forward it, I saw something. A black shadow of a child ran towards the main door of the bank. The one who was recording the video probably ran after the shadow only to find nothing.

The second video was even more terrifying. It was recorded by a young teen girl who sat on the last bench in her class. The video showed the presence of a black figure and when the girl might have turned her phone to record it, the figure might have vanished. Seconds later, when the girl turned to her right, the figure with long, slimy hair and distorted face, was found sitting beside her. The girl must have dropped her phone because the video ended abruptly. Looking at the deadpanned look on my face, Nikhil had a nice time.

'Come on, it was scary. At least these videos confirm that there is something wrong with this village. Don't you think so?'

'I bet you are right,' said Nikhil.

'So, where are we going tonight?'

'Tonight? Don't you mean 'day'?'

'No, I mean 'night'. Such things can be explored and experienced in the darkness of the night. Be ready with torch, candles and matchsticks. Okay?' I asserted.

'But it would be very risky to go out at night. Moreover, if we get caught, nobody will be able to save us- neither from the ghost nor from our parents!' argued Nikhil.

'Nothing will happen, okay? You can ask some of your friends to come with us. That way you will feel better.'

'Okay, I will talk to them,' he sounded uncertain.

Waiting eagerly for the darkness to descend, we finished our dinner and pretended to go to sleep. We had decided to meet outside in the verandah at 11:00 p.m. I met Nikhil and he told me that his friends were waiting for us near the grocery shop. We put all the essential things in a bag and headed out.

'Where do we go from here?' I asked.

'We will go to the haunted cottage and then go and see the tree near Sumerpur Junction,' revealed Nikhil.

A chill ran down my spine. I was excited. Soon excitement was replaced by confusion as one of Nikhil's friends wasn't there.

'Where is Akshay?'

'He didn't come. He is scared and the darkness will make him crazier.' Mayank, one of Nikhil's friends, replied with a smirk.

We proceeded towards the cottage. The air was moist and the beads of sweat were prominent on our forehead.

'What is so special about that cottage, Nikhil?' I asked.

'People say that around 120 years ago, a family lived in this cottage. They all were believers of black magic and probably that's why all of them died a tragic death. Their spirits couldn't be freed and hence, those spirits roam there. One can hear strange sounds as if someone is calling out someone else.' Arjun, another friend of Nikhil, finished in one breath. I could sense the tension in his voice.

'What about the tree?'

'The tree is haunted. Wait till you see it,' Nikhil patted my shoulder and gestured to move on.

I could feel the silence. Even the leaves under our feet could be heard. The only light source was the tiny torch that we had.

In another ten minutes we were standing facing the cottage. Dark and dingy, the old cottage had an iron gate. The main door overlooked a huge yard. Trees thrived on that lonely piece of land. The eerie silence was enough to scare the daylights out of Arjun and Mayank. They looked at Nikhil as if asking to leave but Nikhil stood his ground and motioned them to go ahead. We spotted the staircase that led to the first floor.

'Does a Ramu Kaka live here?' I tried to break the monotony with a lame joke but nobody laughed.

'Don't be a fool. Let's not offend the spirits or else they might attack us and we might die.' Mayank defended.

'Nothing will happen. Let's go inside,' I urged.

The iron gate made a loud creaking noise and that made it quite clear that the gate had not been opened for years. That sound could wake up the entire village! For a millisecond, the thought of my parents catching us scared me but then I brushed aside the thought in a jiffy and focused on what lay ahead. Umpteen number of leaves decorated the yard. They were yellow and jarred. It felt as if they were welcoming us to that hellhole.

Before rotating the doorknob of the front door, Nikhil decided to take a peek through the window but it was too dark to see anything.

'Let's go in. We are simply wasting time outside,' I suggested.

The menacing sound of the doorknob turning in clockwise direction was so loud that we thought our eardrum had been compromised. We moved in and switched on our torch. Other than one large sofa in the center and a relaxing chair by the window, the main hall did not have any significant furniture. We decided to inspect the house by working in teams. While Arjun and I ventured towards the kitchen, Nikhil and Mayank decided to check the other rooms on the ground floor. Suddenly, a loud bang caught us off guard. Something or rather someone had dropped from the ceiling. Without wasting another second, we rushed to be together with the others.

'What was that sound? Did you all hear that?' asked Mayank.

'I don't know but there is something spooky in here. We should hurry and leave,' suggested Nikhil.

'Don't worry. It was just a book,' Arjun clarified holding up the book and flashing it to us.

Relieved, we decided to move to the first floor. A little hesitant, Nikhil did not agree to that easily. It took five minutes to convince him to accompany us upstairs. As we entered the room on the first floor, we were shocked to see a black shadow by the window.

We ran as fast as we could. Fear took toll on our mind and body. Cursing our folly, we kept mumbling that we shouldn't have gone to that place. Fortunately, we were able to escape and heaved a sigh of relief.

We decided to skip the haunted tree as one experience was more than enough. But what Nikhil told us next was a bolt from the blue.

'It will take only one extra left turn to reach the tree. Come on, let's finish seeing it. What do you say, Mahir? Scared already?'

That's the thing about men's ego! When our manhood is at stake, we can brace to face any danger. However, in that situation, I could have let Nikhil have the last laugh. Unfortunately, I didn't.

'Why would I be afraid? Let's go,' I tried to sound confident.

Once near the haunted tree, I suddenly felt an intense pain in my ankle; it had twisted and I eventually fell. I massaged it a bit to soothe the pain but the pain wouldn't go. I looked up to find others and ask them to help me get up. What I saw instead was a woman clad in red saree. Her hair was long and her body was hanging from one of the branches of the tree. To add to the horror, I saw her smile. She wasn't dead, or was she? I had no answer. She was smiling. At me. There was blood on her lips and it dripped, drop by drop.

'Help,' I screamed.

Nikhil and Mayank came running towards me. They didn't waste any time asking irrelevant questions. Maybe they also saw the sight. They helped me get up and carried me to a place where the horror came to a halt.

We didn't talk about it again. Nikhil felt guilty for taking me out to those places but in reality, it was my fault. My curiosity had led to all that. I couldn't sleep that night. Neither could any of the other boys.

We celebrated my grandparents' anniversary and left for Bangalore the next day. While waiting at the Sumerpur junction, my eyes were fixed on the tree and the hanging woman. I just couldn't forget that horrifying sight. When my mother asked me what was wrong, I made up an excuse. I knew that she would first scold me and then refuse to believe me.

Sadly, I am still bearing the brunt of my actions, for the lady in the red saree still haunts me every night. Sleep eludes me and peace of mind seems like a distant dream.

Dreams are like the thin threads of hope

That, if woven together, can give access to the duality.

But often those dreams make it difficult to cope

When they turn into a reality.

TWO DREAMS
~Satyananda Sarangi~

'Home Sweet Home'- the phrase kept ringing in his mind. These three words seemed to associate with two categories of people. One category consisted of the ones who were far away in some aloof land, missing the charms of their dearest motherland. The other comprised of those who, after spending a considerable time outside, were on their return voyage. Akhil was lucky to fall into the latter. His wife was accompanying him on the flight. He wondered how things worked so well between them. She was a renowned professor of Psychology and he was the one of Mathematics, perhaps the only mismatch from his point of view. To add to this, she was a dutiful daughter-in-law, an ideal one, much to the satisfaction of his parents. As fate would have it, they were posted in the same university which gave them ample time to familiarise themselves with each other's likes and dislikes. After working for five years away from their motherland, they had been relocated back to their country recently.

As they took the first few steps into the old street, glimpses of the childhood memories crowded Akhil's mind. It was the same old street where he had grown up, people still flew the kites and children still ran about playing hide and seek. The grocery shop was still in the same place. It had expanded though. There was a larger room and more shelf space. New shops had come up much to his surprise. He never liked them because they hampered the serenity of the place to quite an extent. They neared their house, third from the end, and Akhil winked at his wife saying, 'Here comes your house.' With a killer smile, the one that she often threw at him, she said, 'It's not my house, Akhil, it's ours.' An instantaneous grin was all that he could manage in response.

The house had the same brown nameplate with bold letters of white on it reading 'Mr. Sohan Rajvanshi'. It was his father's name. The name in itself was enough to be recognised in the locality. The primary reason for this was credited to the vocation he was in - the vocation of a judge. No doubt he had retired recently but the product of his hard work stood untainted and undiminished. Akhil rang the doorbell expecting a grand welcome from his mother. However, it was Mr Rajvanshi who opened the door. It seemed as if he was just waiting for their arrival. His hair had more strands of grey but he was still the same - an epitome of sternness- like the head of an Indian family. He said, 'Wait for a minute. Your mother is coming; she is preparing the plate for *Aarti*.'

'Father! Is it needed? We are not a newly-wedded couple,' Akhil asked.

'But you know her and the customs. Do it for her sake,' his father replied. Akhil acceded to his words by shaking his head, a gesture that had remained intact till that day. He had grown up; he had a wife and he was old enough to be a father himself, but it hardly mattered to Mr Rajvanshi. For him, Akhil was the same little kid who had to keep nodding at every word of his. They stood at the entry for a while till his mother emerged. The furrows on her face had augmented and her walking had been slowed down by the effect of time. But time had failed in doing something else; it had failed greatly in weakening the spark of her motherhood. The *aarti* ritual concluded and to everybody's relief, they could go in finally. The afternoon had been very strenuous, so Akhil made up his mind to have a refreshing shower. The shower was good; Akhil engaged in a thorough cleansing of all the fatigue from the body as well as the mind. It was one of those long ones he preferred in that place. The outcome was even longer as he fell asleep immediately after.

It must have been around six when he woke up suddenly due to some noise emanating from the kitchen. It was the sweet conversation between the mother-in-law and daughter-in-law. He stood at the kitchen entrance and stared at both of them. His happiness knew no bounds because his wife and his mother were getting along with each other so well. Grabbing his car keys, he stepped into the garage. The window of the kitchen was right next to the garage. Shouting at the top of his voice, he said, 'I would be back in an hour. All the best and carry on with the gossip.'

Without waiting for any reply, he got into the car and turned on the headlights. He had plans of enjoying a ride to his heart's content.

Akhil had gone for a long drive after many years. The old roads seemed to be his territory. The homecoming had never been so satiating. The swift winds outside the window whispered that they had missed him dearly too. He felt as if the trees were trying to look at him with yearning eyes. Just then, a terrible thought crossed his mind. It wasn't a thought; it was a flashback that conspired to land him into an elapsed phase of life. We, humans, have phases which we wish we could relive; yet some phases we simply wish to run away from. Stopping the car under the vast sky, he was lost in a phase he had tried his best to forget.

Twenty years had passed but that fateful night had settled deep enough to haunt him repeatedly. Akhil was a boy then, hardly thirteen years old. He was away from the worldly wisdom and was possessed by dreams. That was the time when most of the dreams he had in sleep found their way to reality. The good dreams were a bonus, his parents thought. On one such occasion, he had a dream where he was alone in a graveyard. The natural light was fading and he did not have the slightest idea regarding what it was all about. He slowly walked to a tombstone and when he looked at it closely, he felt a hand tapping on his shoulder. He turned back to find his grandmother, the person he was closest to in those days, standing.

Akhil said, 'Thank God, grandma! You are here. Let's get back home.'

'I cannot. This is my new home,' she uttered.

When he woke up, he was on his little bed. His grandmother had not been keeping well for quite a few days. Mr Rajvanshi had tried consulting every doctor in the town but his efforts proved non-productive. Two days later, Akhil's dream came true and his grandmother passed away. His parents were aghast and his father, in particular, was in deep sorrow. Maybe the dream was a greater reason for being upset than his mother's death. Although Akhil was too young to read a mind then, he knew that that event had started to threaten the father-son relationship. With time, the problem took a backseat, for the dreams became infrequent. That sorted some of the problems but the chasm between Mr Rajvanshi and Akhil couldn't be filled.

The horn of another vehicle reminded Akhil that he had stopped midway on his drive. It was 08:00 p.m. and he had to return to the house in time.

The food cooked by his mother had always been his favourite. It was so tasty that he had no control over the consequent burps. Bidding good night to his parents after a sumptuous dinner, his wife and he excused themselves. He never realised when the slumber took over his consciousness.

He could see a well-decorated chamber. There were three huge bookshelves aligned against the walls. A half-opened window was in front of him and he stood with one hand on his hip and the other on a table next to him. A giant pendulum clock hanging on the wall jangled at half-past eleven. A small piece of paper lay on the table under the paperweight. There was a desk calendar next to it. When Akhil glanced at the calendar, something caught his attention; he could hear footsteps. Anxious and scared, he got under the table and positioned himself in such a way that his eyes faced the entrance. The door opened slightly; the person on the other side was trying to know if there was anyone inside.

He had a pair of shabby footwear on; that was the first thing Akhil noticed about him. The man walked in and closed the door behind him. The stranger had an urgency in his steps. Fearing that he might have sensed his presence, Akhil swallowed hard. The man stopped a few inches away from him and turned back. He was holding a dagger. The sharp edge and the shining metal sent a chill down Akhil's spine. The stranger then waited. He waited for someone he was expecting. Just when the door was about to be opened, Akhil felt someone pulling his hand with force. He retaliated and soon realized that he had had another nightmare. It was his wife waking him up.

The dream of that night had left him anxious. Since he had not dreamt anything of that sort for a long time, his mind couldn't let go of it. It was scary. And that left him apprehensive. Trying his best to put up a smiling face, he walked towards the balcony where his wife had arranged the teacups on the table. His mother soon joined him and his wife for tea. She had something in her hand. It was a photo album.

'This is a new one. Do you remember your cousin's wedding party that you missed last year? Here are those pictures and a few more.'

Akhil was overjoyed. He enjoyed every page of it until he came across a particular photograph. It was the one in which Mr Rajvanshi was sitting at a desk. Probably it had been clicked at a new place. He proceeded only to find some more similar ones. The walls in those photographs seemed familiar. 'Ma, which place is this? A new one I guess,' he quizzed her.

Her answer came as a shock to Akhil. Three days went by smoothly. On the fourth morning, Akhil was racing in his car on the national highway. 'I have to get there. But I hope it isn't true anyway,' he mumbled to himself.

Once he entered the area, he couldn't track down the exact address he was looking for. After two helpless rounds, he was finally there where he intended to be. A little later, he was inside the building. His nervousness was getting the better of him. He entered a large room and glanced at every corner of the room.

'Oh my God! I can't believe this,' he said in a panic. It was the same decorated room, the one with the bookshelves and the half-open window that he had seen in his dream. The sight of the big pendulum clock added fuel to his fears. The hands of the clock said that it was half-past eleven. No sooner did he hear the footsteps than the feeling of Déjà vu became stronger. With no other option left, he slipped under the table, and hid in the same manner like he had done in his dream. The stranger was in the room, just a few feet away. The curiosity of seeing the dagger next tickled Akhil's nerves. Once he saw its length, tremors went down his body. He heard someone approaching the door. The assassin was ready to attack and so was Akhil. More than half of his dream had turned into the reality already. Only the last segment remained.

'I should be prepared for anything happening beyond this,' he whispered to himself and began to move slowly. He crawled behind the killer and waited for the visitor. Before the door could open completely, Akhil pounced on the killer and took him by surprise. The dagger fell on the ground beside them. Thinking on his feet, Akhil pushed the dagger with his foot so that it was out of the killer's reach. Akhil and the killer engaged in wrestling. It was quite a sight. Akhil was fierce and landed many blows on the killer's face. The killer was not a weak man either. He, too, landed a couple of blows on the Akhil's abdomen.

Just then, somebody got in. It was Mr Rajvanshi. That was his new office building, the place where he used to meet his clients even after retirement.

'What the hell are you doing here? Who is this stranger?' he screamed.

'Hold on, father,' saying this Akhil caught the man who had already inflicted several blows on him by then. He had to pay him back. Akhil punched him, kicked him severely until he was on the ground. The police had been already informed by Akhil. They reached just in the nick of time and arrested the killer.

A long impending hug was next. Mr Rajvanshi was emotional and he let out his feelings in the form of an embrace. That was the first time after Akhil's grandmother's death that Mr Rajvanshi had hugged him.

That afternoon, when they reached home, Mr Rajvanshi said to his wife, 'Your son's gift of precognition gifted me another life today.'

Turning to his son, he queried, 'Tell me one thing. How did you know that my life was at risk?'

'It's a long story, father. If I tell you, you won't believe me,' replied Akhil.

'Umm… I still want to know,' said Mr Rajvanshi.

Akhil began, 'A weird dream started it all. That was on the first night after I came here.'

He narrated the entire nightmare to his father, who listened to him very carefully.

'Why didn't you tell me anything about this?' asked his father.

'It wasn't real, father. It was an ordinary event seen by my subconscious mind. I had decided to take it lightly but when mother showed me the photo album, I knew that it couldn't just be a dream,' Akhil replied.

'Which one? The new one?'

'Yes, that's the one. It had some pictures of you inside the renovated office. The clock, the walls and the bookshelves were recognised by me instantly. It was then that I became serious. Still, I couldn't locate the place. I didn't ask mother, for she would have become stressed. I wasn't even sure if all that would come true. Since I didn't want to take any risk, I left no stone unturned in finding out more about it. Do you remember that I mentioned about the piece of paper, a visiting card I think, that lay under the paperweight in your office in my dream?' he sought his father's confirmation to go ahead.

'Yes, I do. But why does the card come into picture here?' Mr Rajvanshi spoke with inquisitiveness.

'I didn't know what it was then but perhaps God had other plans. For some reason, the numbers on that paper were clear in my memory. I knew that you could have left the card on your desk only if you were expecting that person to visit you next. In the dream, the one who came in next was the assassin. So, I dialled those digits to find out the owner of that number.'

'How did you manage to get the name of the person who had that number?' his father asked, now excited about how the events were unfolding.

'I have a school friend of mine who works in the Telecom department. I contacted him to help me. He revealed that the number belonged to Mr Desai, the famous industrialist. Now, the big question was *what grudge did Mr Desai have against you?* I had to find out.'

Mr Rajvanshi interrupted him, 'We haven't met in person yet.'

With a deep sigh, Akhil resumed, 'I didn't know this person. To get to the bottom of the truth, I needed to get hold of your recent case files. Apologies for that, but I had to do it without your knowledge. I went through most of them without success. There was not even the slightest hint of Mr Desai! I decided to visit him the next day. He was out of the station, his security guard told me. His car was parked and the driver was leaning onto it. He looked familiar. I figured out that the driver's photograph was in one of your case files. I rushed home to confirm my doubt and it was true. The particular file stated that the driver was the brother of an accused, who had been sentenced for life imprisonment. You had won the case for a client of yours. Everything became clear. The driver had made up a perfect plan to avenge his brother's imprisonment. He had decided to use his boss' identity. I kept a close watch on him for a day. This morning, I followed him to your office, and father, you know the rest.'

'You could have lodged a complaint with the police beforehand. Why didn't you?' Mr Rajvanshi retorted.

'A dream can neither be the reason behind police's action nor be used as a piece of evidence for the prosecution of the law,' Akhil remarked.

His father opened his mouth in amazement. 'Point noted, Mr Junior Rajvanshi. That's why your mother always insisted that you become a detective while I kept scolding you for watching those underrated detective shows. But my son, I am a proud father now,' he ended with a smile.

Akhil's heart had been freed from a lingering burden. One dream had distanced him from his father and another one had helped him reconcile with his father. The long-lasting guilt in him had been washed away owing to one cryptic encounter in his dream!

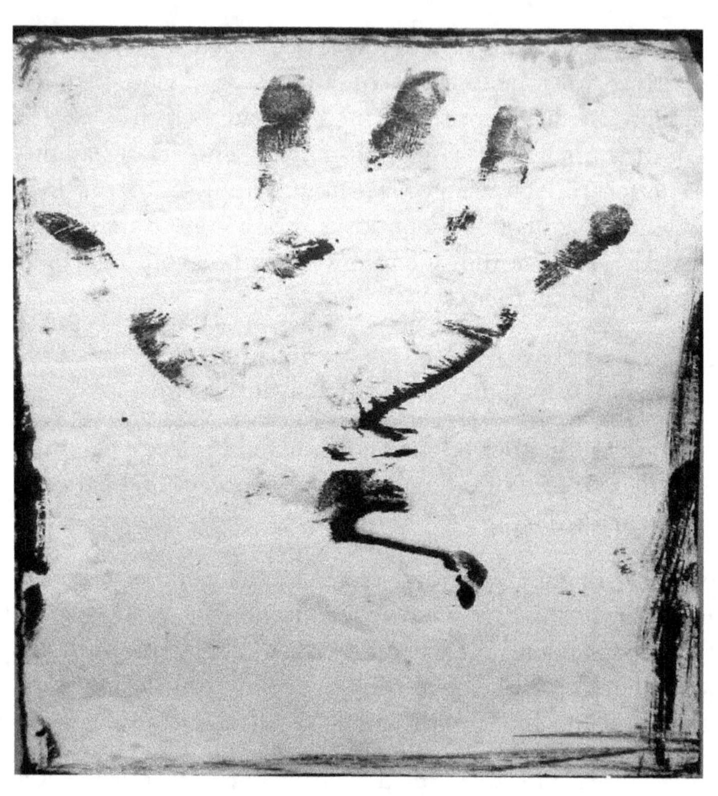

The huge mountain and the long trail

Often whisper to each other at night.

'Again, the men and the spirits are having ale

But soon they will know that things aren't alright!'

LEH'D FOREVER
~Sid Stevens~

Bike ride in Leh is every bachelor's dream. You cannot really die at peace unless you've checked it off your bucket list. The mesmerizing mountains beckon you to explore one of the toughest places inhabited by man. There is a silent calling that pulls you every time you see somebody's picture on Instagram or Facebook, showing-off their excursion. I was no exception. However, I did not think even in my wildest imagination that the trip to Leh would leave me marked for life.

The flight landed in Leh at 0630 hrs and I could barely contain my excitement. The airport was a small one- but in no possible way I can say that it had less facilities compared to the airports in the Metro cities. The wait near the luggage belt was brief and before I knew it, I was in the cab heading to the hotel. Like a child in a fairyland, I stuck my neck out of the window. I wanted to absorb it all, I had to. It was beautiful, serene and unadulterated. Underpopulated and quiet, the city of Leh welcomed me with its open arms! The long stretch of the road with nothing to obscure the mountain view looked enticing. Those red giants made me realise how small and impermanent my stature in this universe was. Philosophical thoughts continued the Zumba in my mind till I reached my hotel. It was a small hotel – more like a hostel or dormitory with shared rooms and common toilets. The old gentleman at the reception gave me the keys wishing me a pleasant stay. It had been a tiresome night due to the connecting flights from Mumbai to Leh with a layover in Delhi. I could feel the need for acclimatisation as the thin air made me pant on my way up the stairs.

'Hi, my name is Mehul,' introduced the boy in the room, offering his hand as I entered.

'Hi, I am Sid, well Siddharth I mean.' I replied shaking his firm hand.

I glanced at my room which had two single beds, two small tables and a small wall mounted TV. There was just enough room left to walk and reach the furniture. I placed my rucksack under the bed and hopped on the bed. Over the next fifteen minutes, I exchanged notes with Mehul and we weren't strangers anymore. Mehul was from Delhi and had arrived there five days earlier. That day was his last day before he set course home.

Mehul was a regular boy-next-door – enthusiastic, cheerful and outspoken. Guessing by his appearance and interests, I could safely conclude that he was of my age and that was the reason we hit it off quite well.

'I've already explored the Nubra Valley with double humped camels and have been to the famous monastery called Diskit Gompa. Leh market is not too great if you ask me.' Mehul said pointing at my itinerary sheet.

'Did you do it all in a hired cab?'

'Yes.'

'Why?' I asked him, genuinely surprised.

'Well, I am not too comfortable with the idea of riding alone here. What if something goes wrong? Help will be miles away,' he said. The genuine concern for life was quite evident in his tone.

I scoffed at his idea and proudly explained my grand plan of exploring it all on a Royal Enfield. I told him about how I had always dreamt of riding like the Ghost Rider of those comics and TV shows.

'Mehul, I see that you have kept the famous Pangong Tso lake for the last – for today. Even I intended to do that on the last day of my trip. But if you are game, I'll change my plan. Let's hire the bike and you ride with me as my wingman. It'll be fun. As such you are never going to come again here just for a bike ride. Right?' I tried to sound convincing.

'I don't know. Cab sure seems a much safer option. But I'm not coming again to Leh, that's a valid point you've made,' he replied poking the lines on his forehead.

'C'mon now. Don't overthink it. Life is too short to ponder and waste. Let me make your last day in Leh the most memorable one. You will neither regret it nor forget it your whole life.' I stated as if delivering a lecture on philosophy.

--***--

By 1000hrs, we had rented a Royal Enfield and tied our bags behind. As I donned my helmet, the nerd in me showed off, 'Mehul, do you know that The Royal Enfield Classic 350 is powered by a 346cc, single-cylinder air-cooled engine?'

'I've absolutely no idea what that means. Just don't drop me,' he responded and we both laughed.

It was an amazing ride. The lonely road seemed to stretch out to infinity with gigantic mountains on either side. The lack of vegetation and the red hue around them gave the surroundings a nostalgic touch. Pelting at 90-100kmph on that beast, we could hear wind noise in our helmets. Our first stop was the famous Magnetic hill. It was said that objects moved against the gravity due to the magnetic pull of the hill. We stopped the bike at the signboard and waited. Nothing happened. That did not deter us from cherishing a few gulps of water and taking a selfie with the signboard before moving on in the opposite direction, for Pangong was not in the direction of the Magnetic Hill.

We passed by the highest LPG bottling plant in the world and took a picture to save as a souvenir. While I was busy driving, Mehul clawed my shoulder.

'Stop. Stop. Look over there,' he said pointing towards the beautiful river. It was far beyond the cliff we were standing on. It was pristine.

'That's the Indus river. People used to do rafting over there until last year. It was supposed to be great fun. I have heard that the rapids there are quite good. Only if it was allowed, we could have done that as well,' sighed Mehul.

'Why isn't it allowed now?' I inquired.

'Last year, a raft toppled and a couple of boys drowned. Thereafter, the authorities shut it down. It was all over the local media. You can Google it for details.' Mehul explained.

'Whatever man! We are missing out on a fun activity due to some reckless fools. At least we should save the memory that we were here.' I suggested.

Mehul smiled and we clicked our third selfie.

After three hour's ride, we reached Chang-La pass – the second highest pass in the world. A selfie with hot Maggie at the local *dhaba* – it was another tick on our itinerary. Our next stop was supposed to be the Pangong Tso lake and we knew that the ride would be long.

Over the next two hours, we crossed the Sakti Nagar Valley which was a lush green expanse, like an oasis out of nowhere in that dry land. As we rode up the mountain, the roads zigzagged like in a labyrinth. We saluted as we passed several army trucks. We gaped in awe as the road turned to stones and pebbles with sand-brick walls on either side giving the track the appearance of an Egyptian styled cave. We clicked several photographs capturing these picturesque scenes before reaching the lake.

The first view of the lake was truly breath-taking. The water had five different shades of blue and 60 percent of it was in China – the local shopkeeper told us. All the fatigue vanished as we dipped our feet in the cold water of the Pangong Lake. We sat on the side, tossing pebbles like children, counting the number of hops they made before sinking. The vendors came there from nearby village during the day and returned by evening. We clicked several pictures and ordered tea and Maggi.

'It's beautiful, isn't it, Sid?' Mehul asked.

'It's awesome. I would have never wanted to miss this. The entire trip is incomplete without it,' I said sipping my tea.

'Precisely. Even though the six-hour journey felt like crossing the world, I would have definitely regretted had I not visited this place.' Mehul laughed.

It was about 1700hrs already and we wanted to reach back as soon as possible. We spent another half an hour at the lake and started our journey back. As we crossed Indus river rafting point, the sad accident clouded my mind again and I felt sorry for the poor boys who lost their lives. The long ride turned colder as the sun dipped and disappeared. For the first time, the wisdom of Mehul's words dawned upon me and I felt a bit scared. Another hour and we'd be back, I told myself. To keep fears at bay, both of us started singing the popular Bollywood track *"Tanha Dil Tanha Safar"* by Shaan. Our bonding made me forget that we had met just a few hours ago. The Magnetic Hill wasn't that far from our hotel. Thus, we decided to give it another try.

'Let's give it another shot, Sid. Maybe it works this time. Who is coming here again, right?' he gestured towards the spot where we had parked our bike earlier. His voice sounded more resolute than before.

Honestly, I wasn't sure and was even a little scared. It was dark all around and the howling wind sounded ominous. But I couldn't expose my fears to the dude — too much pride there! 'Of course, Of course! Why not!' I nodded in affirmation.

We placed the bottle horizontally on the same spot as before and waited – nothing.

'It's all a hoax. Let's go.' Saying that I turned to face our bikes.

'Wait, Sid. Look!' Mehul's excitement was contagious.

I don't know if it was our tired eyes, the darkness playing tricks or the adrenaline causing hallucination, but I could see the bottle roll.

As Mehul clapped in excitement, I struggled to find my voice. I think I forced a "Wow" out of my mouth before jumping onto the bike.

'All right Mr. Johnny Bravo, just one selfie,' Mehul said, clearly amused at my lack of bravado. I don't think it was my phone's flashlight that made my face look white at that time. I kicked the Enfield royally and we sped towards our hotel.

It was almost 2330hrs when we reached the hotel. We were greeted by a couple of street dogs who started barking at our sight. Mehul went to get some cash while I went up to our room and ordered dinner. We were super tired as we lay on our beds that night. We talked about the crazy ride and the awesome day that we had had. I never knew when sleep engulfed me. That night I dreamt of flying over the river, the lake and the Magnetic hill.

Next morning, I found a note by my bedside from Mehul.

'Hi, Sid. Thanks a lot for making my last day here so adventurous and helping me complete my trip. It was a long due wish come true. I am sorry but I had to leave early. Take care.'

I returned to Mumbai after completing the trip exactly as was done by Mehul. It was a good trip but I had missed his company during the next 5 days. Nostalgia took over as I switched on my laptop to transfer the pictures and relive the memories. The experiences had become memories now. The folder was named "Leh'd" and it made me smile. I scanned through the pictures and I could feel the adrenaline rush. The pounding of heart and the increased blood flow made my senses tingle. Memories flooded my mind as I dialled Mehul's mobile number. In my mind, I was grateful for the moment when we had exchanged phone numbers.

'Yes. Who's is this?' answered a lady.

'Aunty, my name is Sid. I met Mehul in Leh five days back and we had a good time together. Can I please speak to him?' I asked, rubbing my forehead.

'Is this some kind of a joke?' rebuked the lady on the other side.

'Joke? Why would this be a joke, aunty?'

'Mehul has been dead for over a year now. He had gone to Leh last year and had drowned in a rafting accident. Do you think it is nice to prank call and disturb a grieving family?'

I dropped the phone. I was too stunned to be able to speak. My ears rang as I looked at the laptop screen. All those selfies had nobody else but me. I held the handwritten note by Mehul and the irony of my own words echoed -

"Life is too short to ponder and waste. Let me make your last day at Leh the most memorable one. You will neither regret it nor forget it your whole life."

The lurking faceless shadows during the night

Often deprive me of the sleep and change my plight.

I am left scared and scarred-

The hope of looking for light is always marred.

THAT ONE NIGHT
~Soumya Sarita Kar~

I was sitting in the last room on the third floor of the hotel. It was early in the evening when I reached Bhopal and within minutes, I was able to check into the hotel. I had gone there to present a paper in a three-day international conference organized by the Department of Archaeology. I was one of the invited professors and I had to stay in Bhopal for two days in Hotel Regalia.

After a quick shower, I relaxed on the spotless feather-soft bed. The interior of the room reflected the palatial taste of the interior designer. After all, they did take good care of the customers' interest. Within seconds, I fell asleep. I was contented with my place of stay; it was both comfortable and classy.

Suddenly, a loud noise woke me up. I checked the time; it was already half-past eight and I realised that I had slept for two hours. I got ready within ten minutes to go out for dinner, for I always preferred to have my food outside to be able to taste the local cuisine.

After walking for ten minutes, I checked into a not-so-small restaurant and ordered my all-time favourite Butter Naan and Mushroom Masala. Post my dinner, I engaged in a casual conversation with the waiter, a young boy of nineteen perhaps. I like to talk to the denizens, for it allows me to feel connected to the new place. It doesn't matter whether they are the shopkeepers, tea-sellers, waiters or receptionists. When he discovered that I was staying in the Hotel Regalia, his eyes widened.

'Are you staying in that hotel, sir? Which room? Is this your first visit to Bhopal?' asked the boy whose name was Nitesh. Fear and tension were evident on his forehead.

'Why? What's wrong with staying there? Is that not a genuine place? But it looks so nice and well-maintained.' I shot an array of questions at him. I had read the reviews and then agreed for that hotel. My decision couldn't have been wrong!

The waiter gestured towards the man sitting at the payment counter and asked me to talk to him about the hotel.

'What is wrong with Hotel Regalia?' I asked.

He hesitated but then spoke, 'One of the rooms is believed to be haunted by a rigid spirit. Nobody knows which room it is because the staff never gives out any information that would taint their reputation. Those who have been living here never dare to step into that hotel, leave alone asking about the room!'

Being more pragmatic and logical, I refused to believe what he said. I paid the amount and returned to my room. Probably one of the reasons why I didn't believe him was because I was in a profession where only logical reasoning worked. I freshened up and switched on the television. I didn't feel like watching. The soothing weather called me outside. I felt like sitting on the balcony for some time. Sleep was nowhere around me.

The unaccustomed feeling of hollowness engulfed my being. The hotel premise was dark. Shadows perched on the walls. I sat facing the garden but nothing was visible. I felt uneasy and couldn't find out the reason. Some kind of strange, gloomy and unidentifiable feeling kept bothering me. The change in the temperature of the wind could be felt by my skin. While at one point the soothing wind would caress my cheek, the very next instant, the warm wind would thrash my other cheek. I had not experienced anything of that kind earlier. Giving up the idea of sitting there, I went back inside, sat on my bed and switched on my laptop. I thought of going through the paper once more. That way, I would be better prepared.

It took me another hour to go through the entire paper, following which I stretched my legs, turned off the laptop and adjusted the light of the bed lamp. I felt that my feet were swollen and soon realised that it was the aftereffect of the long journey. I was so desperately in need of a long and sound sleep that I pulled the quilt to my chest and within a minute, I fell asleep.

The loud knock on my door woke me up. I felt I had been thrown off my bed. That was strange. Cursing my mind and assuming it to be a dream, I buried my head in my pillow and went back to sleeping. But that was just the beginning. After a few minutes, the loud incessant knock on the door startled me. That time, I could not help but get up because I was sure that someone was at the door. Wondering who it could be, I checked the time. It was quarter past one. 'Who could be there at this hour?' I asked no one in particular. The knocking became louder. A chill ran down my spine. My palms became sweaty and my throat cried for water.

'Who is there?' I asked in a sceptical voice but there was no reply. I rose, tiptoed towards the door and rested one ear on it. I don't know why I tiptoed towards the door. My intellectual mind also refused to argue the toss, for the situation at hand was tenser than it seemed. I did not hear any noise thereafter. Just to be sure, I asked once again, 'Who is there?' Nobody responded. Irritated, I cursed the perturbing situation and headed back to the bed. The moment I switched the lights off, I heard the tap of pointed heels near the door. I became a little careful the second time and without any prior warning, I opened the door but found no one there. Suddenly a gust of chilled wind collided with my face. I was shocked to find that the entire corridor was illuminated bright and there was no trace of any animate existence at all. I closed the door and tried to understand what was going on. I was so tired of dealing with such unanticipated things that I muttered vaguely and threw myself on the bed almost in despair. Hoping that I would be able to sleep peacefully at that time, I shut my eyes. But there was no respite in store.

(After several minutes or so)

Someone whispered near my ear. There was something heavy and cold on my chest. Subconsciously, I pulled the blanket up to my chin but seconds later, I felt the same. I tried to remove the invisible heavy object from my chest. To my horror, I saw a hand- as pale as death, as cold as ice. Shivering and sweating, I tried to lift the hand from my chest but it was strong, so strong that it pushed me back on the flat surface of the bed. I was incapacitated. I couldn't lift myself. Desperate and helpless, I opened my mouth to shout but it had turned voiceless out of shock and horror. Gradually, the icy cold hand reached my throat and pressed it. I couldn't think of anything; my mind was numb. Fortunately, my hand hit the switch of the bed lamp while I was struggling to escape the clutches of the unknown force. The moment the light was switched on, the emptiness was back. The hand had vanished and there seemed to be no one present other than me. The unbearable heaviness was gone too.

Gasping heavily to catch my breath, I gulped a whole glass of water and rushed to the washroom to wash my sweaty face. While wiping my face, I noticed a silhouette sliding past the garden; it later dissolved into the darkness of the nearby woods. I couldn't fathom what had happened with me a few minutes back. Was it a dream or was it all real? I had no answers. I could recall what the waiter and the man at the money counter had warned me about. Goosebumps appeared on my skin and I immediately rang up the reception. The phone was picked up but I could hear only vague whispering followed by enraged muttering. My head started spinning and soon I collapsed on the bed.

In the morning, I woke up on the floor, exhausted and confused, as if I had woken up from a dream. Only a minute later, I realised that I could no longer stay in that hotel as the horrifying encounter of the previous night came rushing back to my mind. I recalled the paranormal activities; my scratched body was proof. I was no more in the state of ignoring the presence. No matter what I believed in and what I was, I had to pack my bags and leave before things became worse. I packed my things and headed to the University to attend the conference. I checked out of the hotel that morning. The receptionist did give me a confused look but I was determined about not spending another minute in that hellhole. I spent the remaining day travelling to different places but could not enjoy at all owing to that incident. I returned to my hometown hoping that I would leave the bag of bad memories behind but it did not happen.

Every night the shadow reappears. But it never actually comes out of my dream.

Blood, flowers, cherries and wine

Red is the colour of life and fine dine.

But when anger takes control of the mind

Red can make a demon of mankind!

THE RED WINE
~Sreya Mukherjee~

'Finally, the day has arrived,' Andrew smugly mused. No, it wasn't his birthday that day; or perhaps by a contorted logic, one can say that it was. After all, wasn't this day destined to usher a new phase in Andrew's life? That day would bestow a new lease of life to him; hence, one would be justified in calling it his birthday.

The beeping of his phone pulled him out of his reverie. It was a message from Ajay, his colleague from the office. It read, 'Congratulations! I want a grand party. Don't give any excuses. And don't forget your hapless friend once you fly off to America.' Andrew smiled indulgently as it was evident that Ajay adored him. Almost all of his colleagues admired and adored him. Andrew's charismatic personality, coupled with his good looks and pleasant disposition, won him a great many friends and admirers. However, this deluge of admiration had deluded him into thinking that the world revolved around him. But in that case, it wasn't presumptuous of him to think that for the last few days he had become the hot topic of discussion amongst his colleagues. Rumours had it that the managerial board had decided to promote him and offer him a position in their San Francisco branch. There were several other perks such as furnished and luxurious accommodation, subsidised transportation, free gym membership, etc. His performance had been excellent in the last fiscal year and he had been expecting an appraisal but the promotion was beyond his wildest imagination. He had always been attracted to the idea of living in America and making a living but being a mediocre student, he had accepted the harsh truth that that dream would forever remain unfulfilled.

'Now all my dreams will be fulfilled for Lady Luck has finally smiled upon me,' Andrew gloated as he chewed on his breakfast. That day, his manager was supposed to officially declare his promotion and offer him the transfer letter to the U.S.A. Andrew had already prepared the speech which he would deliver after the official announcement. He had meticulously planned every moment of the day; he wanted the day to be perfect and ensured that nothing went awry. He put on his best suit, wore his most charming smile and set out for the office. 'It will be the best day of my life,' he kept chanting.

He got stuck in traffic and that spoiled his mood a bit. But no adversity seemed strong enough to dampen his euphoria. Soon, he was immersed in the joy of receiving appreciation in front of everybody. Late owing to traffic, he was compelled to rush through the office lobby to mark his attendance. As he was rushing, he collided with a colleague which made him almost topple though he regained his balance in the nick of time. But his colleague was not as lucky as him as she couldn't save herself from the impact of the collision. She lay supine on the floor. Her satchel flew open scattering all its contents on the lobby floor. Andrew felt sorry for her and extended his hand to help her but the moment he saw her face, he instantly withdrew his hand. It was Shalini, the most despised colleague. Though there was no concrete reason for Andrew to despise Shalini yet he couldn't help hating her. Perhaps it was Andrew's bloated ego that could not accept Shalini's indifference towards him. She was the only person in his office who didn't pander to his pompous self-image and made no effort at being his friend. However, Shalini wasn't indifferent particularly to Andrew; it was her reclusive nature which made her indifferent to people in general. She had no friends in office and wasn't at all bothered by it. She was happy to lead a solitary life.

'Next time, try to make more effective use of your eyes,' Andrew growled and left her lying on the floor with her files and papers scattered all around.

As he fiddled with the paperweight on his desk, he found himself pondering over the mishap in the lobby. Andrew was incensed at the imperfect beginning of his perfect day, more so because it was with Shalini that he had collided. The thought of Shalini not only riled him up but also made him anxious. Just as she ruined the beginning, she also posed a threat of devastating his entire 'perfect' day. That was not merely Andrew's unfounded anxiety; it had a solid foundation of truth in it. Andrew's promotion and his realization of the Dream Job was not as smooth a ride as he and his colleagues made it out to be. The news of that anticipated promotion had more to it which Andrew deliberately ignored; it was only the partial news that he chose to believe. Yet his wilful ignorance didn't change the fact that the managerial board decided upon two candidates who were being considered for the promotion; one was Andrew and the other was Shalini. Andrew and all his colleagues believed that Shalini stood no chance of being preferred over Andrew. Shalini was a recluse and hardly made any effort to please the boss, while Andrew made an all-out effort to charm the boss and was a favoured employee amongst the managerial board. Though all the odds were in Andrew's favour yet it didn't eliminate Shalini from the race. She had a minuscule chance of winning the race but the fact that she was in the race made Andrew anxious.

As the day progressed, his anxiety increased; he didn't hear anything from the boss neither did Shalini. In a way, no news was good news. That soothed his frayed nerves. After the lunch-break, Andrew received a call from the boss asking him to come to his cabin immediately. Andrew surreptitiously eyed Shalini to check whether she was also going to the boss' cabin. As he saw her immersed in her work, he was ensured that she had not received any call from the boss. Thus, heaving a sigh of relief, he made his way to the boss' cabin.

Walking out of the cabin, he found the attention of all his colleagues riveted upon him, their eyes lit with anticipation. Before he could utter a word, Ajay rushed and embraced him. He wanted to outdo everyone else in congratulating Andrew but he met with an unexpected response. Andrew pushed him away and started laughing maniacally before he crumbled onto the floor bawling. Everyone was perturbed by his sudden maniac behaviour but no one could muster the courage to approach him. After what seemed like an eternity, he finally cooled down and regained his composure. His eyes were bloodshot red and he shot a glance of pure hatred towards Shalini who was still immersed in her work, unperturbed by the drama unfolding around her. He shouted menacingly, 'Congratulations, witch! You have succeeded in snatching away my dreams with your black magic.'

Without taking her eyes off her computer screen, Shalini calmly replied, 'I think you have forgotten that along with you, I was also being considered for promotion. It isn't gracious of you to blame me if the managerial board has chosen me over you, is it?'

The entire office was dumbstruck to hear that it was Shalini who had been promoted and not Andrew. Andrew retorted with equal composure, 'Yes, it isn't gracious of me to blame you. Why don't you prove your graciousness by inviting us all for dinner at your house? I suppose with this undeserved promotion you can finally afford to regale us, can't you?'

Looking away from her computer screen, Shalini answered with a sigh, 'Yes, owing to my *undeserved* promotion, I can finally afford to throw a party. So, I invite all of you for dinner at my home tonight. Andrew, you would be my guest of honour. Please be there at 8 p.m. Don't disappoint me.'

Though no one could comprehend the rationale behind Andrew's asking for a party from Shalini, yet everyone was intrigued by the interesting turn of the events. Shalini was an enigma to everyone. Neither had she ever visited anyone's house nor had she invited anyone to her house. It was only when they saw Andrew's message in the WhatsApp group did they realize the importance of the occasion. Andrew had some faint idea that Shalini lived in a dilapidated dwelling in the less privileged part of the city. He provoked her into inviting them all to her house because he wanted to make fun of her poor living standards. It was his only way of venting his anger at what he believed was a grossly unjust decision of the managerial board. Thus, he wanted all his colleagues to support him in mocking and insulting Shalini. Though it seemed like a mean and petty idea, yet all of them agreed to oblige Andrew because they too believed that Andrew had been wronged.

As they reached Shalini's house, they discovered that she, indeed, lived in a dilapidated and barely furnished apartment. Nevertheless, she made magnificent arrangements to entertain her guests. She had placed a huge stereo on a table with an eclectic collection of music tapes and had asked her guests to select the music of their choice. She had prepared delectable dishes and had an abundant supply of snacks and wine to keep her guests occupied and satiate their taste buds. Unexpectedly, the guests found themselves enjoying and she turned out to be a good host. Andrew was infuriated to see everyone praising Shalini and having a gala time. He felt that the whole purpose of asking for the party was defeated. He felt compelled to salvage the situation and take revenge from the one person who had snatched his dream of going to America.

Suddenly, Andrew turned off the stereo forcing the room into a stunned silence. The silence was rent as he jeered, 'Shalini, what an inattentive host you are! Have you noticed that the empty wine bottle has not yet been replenished? Or are you being your usual parsimonious self and saving the wine by not serving it to the guests?' His friends, taking the cue, also joined him in an uproarious demand of wine.

Shalini answered composedly, 'Despite my earnest efforts, I know I have failed as a host but I beg all of you to bear with me. I think you all can see that I have no one to help me and I have to manage everything single-handedly. Yes, I have been inattentive; I should have replenished the wine bottle earlier but I was busy laying out the table for dinner. However, I won't keep you all waiting any longer. Andrew, it will be very kind of you if you accompany me to the kitchen and help me carry the wine glasses. Meanwhile, you all can enjoy. Please, don't let this minor inconvenience spoil the fun.'

She threw a beseeching glance at Andrew before leaving the room. Andrew stood undecided for a moment before hesitatingly following her into the kitchen.

She returned after a long time carrying a tray of glasses filled with red wine. However, Andrew was nowhere to be seen which made his friends a little uncomfortable. 'Where is Andrew?' asked Ajay.

'Please, have more wine. I am sure you will enjoy it. It is the finest you can find here. And this time, there will be no delay in replenishing once you finish it,' she spoke and passed the glasses to the guests.

A few of them took a hesitant sip and immediately spat it out. 'What the hell is this?' asked one of them.

Shalini flashed a dazzling smile and replied, 'I ran out of the wine, so I thought Andrew's blood will make an excellent replacement. Thus, I pried open his stomach and filled the glasses. Isn't it the finest red wine that you have ever had? Please, enjoy your drinks.'

MEET THE AUTHORS

ALAN DEROSBY

Alan Derosby, a Maine native, has spent the past several years focusing on his passion: writing. Alan has created original and spooky short stories, having THE GHOST AT OLD MILL'S PUB and WINDOWSILL published online as well as four in print anthologies, titled GOING HOME, FULL MOON, KUNK, and UNDER THE BED. Six more short stories are to be published by the end of the year. He has made it to the second round of the Amazon Breakthrough Novel awards with his young historical fiction novel *Lost Souls of Purgatory*.

When not writing, Alan is teaching history at Messalonskee High School in Oakland, Maine, spending time with his family, or watching the New York Mets win the World Series; hopefully.

Instagram: /aderosby75

Facebook: /ADerosbyauthor

AVIJIT ROY

Avijit Roy was born in West Bengal, India. He got his degree in English Literature from Calcutta University. At present, he is a teacher in a high school in his native state. His first published book is "Sela, the River Princess" (2019). His other published books are "Children of a Whimsical God", "A Late Sunrise", "Pictorial Biography of William Shakespeare", "A Return Gift for Santa" and "Wings of Dreams". His stories have been published in international magazines like 'WINK', 'Pangolin Review', 'Breaking Rule Publisher', 'Brilliant Flash Fiction' and 'Inner Child Press'.

Facebook: /Avijit-Roy-author

BISWADEEP GHOSH HAZRA

Biswadeep Ghosh Hazra has worked as a Software Tester/Quality Engineer in Tech Mahindra, Hyderabad, and as a content writer and manager in a company called ExamFocus. He is now studying Business Management (BM) at Xavier Institute of Management, Bhubaneswar. Biswadeep has a passion for writing poetry, short stories, novellas and plays and has published his works in various national and international magazines, books and journals. He has more than nine years of experience in content writing (articles, web contents, brochures, marketing materials, for a multitude of companies, websites).

Facebook: /biswadeep.g.hazra

DESMOND WHITE

Desmond White is a speculative fiction writer who resides in Colorado. He is the editor-in-chief of Rune Bear and an assistant editor at Coffin Bell. His contributions to the horror genre include a speculative murder mystery published in Flame Tree Publishing's Gothic Fantasy series.

Instagram: /desmondwrite

Facebook: /desmondwrite

GUNJAN RATHORE

Gunjan Rathore is a meticulous student who believes in the motto of ask-believe-receive. She is a graduate pursuing CA Finals and CS Executive and was the school topper in the boards. She has been a keen reader since her childhood and started writing at the age of twelve. Writing invigorates her. She owns a page on Instagram that comprises of motivational posts and one-liners. Her hobbies are dancing, singing and playing guitar.

Instagram: /Pensive_writing

Facebook: /gunjan.rathore.5011

KUMAR VIKRANT

Kumar Vikrant is a post graduate in English literature. He is a public servant under state government of Uttar Pradesh. His first published story was, 'Progeny,' which he wrote for the anthology, '31 Sins.' After it, he wrote more than hundred stories for several anthologies.

'The Notebook Of Romance,' 'Winged Hearts,' 'Case Files Of The Dead,' 'The Fallen Angels,' 'Stri,' 'Cupid Calls, 'Love You Mother Nature,' 'It's All About Dogs & Bitches, 'Flavours of India,' 'Unbounded Trajectories,' 'Crumpled Voices 3,' 'Knitted Narratives,' are some of the few anthologies which feature his stories. He has also edited 'Frozen Emotion- A Casket of Broken Strings'.

Facebook: /kumar.vik.1

Michael J Moore

Michael J Moore lives with his wife, author Cait Moore, in Seattle, Washington. His books include Highway Twenty, which appeared on the Preliminary Ballot for the Bram Stoker Award, the bestselling post-apocalyptic novel After the Change, which is used as curriculum at the University of Washington and the psychological thriller Secret Harbor. His work has received awards, has appeared in various anthologies, journals, magazines, newspapers (including The Huffington Post) and has been adapted for theatre.

Instagram: /michaeljmoorewriting

Facebook: /michaeljmoorewriting

SAMRAT SAHU

Samrat is a 27-year-old who works in a government bank. He has studied Engineering. Having participated in 5 anthologies so far, he believes that nothing happens without a reason. He spends him time reading books, playing cricket. He likes to sing as well.

Instagram: /Samrat.rks

Facebook: /Samratsahu

SATYANANDA SARANGI

Satyananda Sarangi is a civil servant by profession. Being an electrical engineer alumnus of IGIT Sarang, he is a young poet, short story teller and an editor who enjoys reading Longfellow, Shelley, Coleridge, Yeats, Blake and many others. His works have been widely published in India, Germany and the United States. His poems have been featured in The Society of Classical Poets, Page & Spine, Glass: Facets of Poetry, WestWard Quarterly, The GreenSilk Journal and other international magazines and books. He served as one of the editors of the non-fiction project "Meri Kahani". Currently, he resides in Odisha, India.

Facebook: /satyananda.sarangi

SID STEVENS

Sid is a beloved husband and doting father of two princesses. An aviator by profession, he loves to soar high above the clouds giving wings to his imagination-literally. He loves travelling through pages and places and loves to discover the beautiful worlds of present, past and fiction.

He believes and quotes-

"There are countless expressions to a single thought. Poetry flows endlessly through pages and time and the romance continues."

He is madly in love with his verses and his wife.

Instagram: /sid.stevens

Facebook: /SidStevens

SOUMYA SARITA KAR

Soumya hails from Cuttack, Odisha. Besides Odia, she can speak, read and write in English, Hindi and French. She is a lecturer. Being a Literature scholar, she has a great inclination towards literature which paved her way to pour out her heart and emotions on paper. She loves to read as well as write poems and short stories.

Instagram: /ssoumya_sarita_65

Facebook: /SoumyasaritaKar

SREYA MUKHERJEE

Sreya Mukherjee has completed her graduation (English) from Banaras Hindu University. Currently, she is pursuing her master's degree in English Literature from English and Foreign Languages University, Hyderabad. She is an inquisitive woman with an insidious tendency of poking into the surface of the accepted narratives. Her ambit of interests is expansive, ranging from languages to occult studies to quantum physics. She is an avid reader and likes to capture the world around her and the vivid one in her mind through words.

Instagram: /shakespeare_chic

Shannon Elizabeth Gardner

Shannon Elizabeth Gardner is a graduate from the University of Wisconsin - Stevens Point with a Bachelor's degree in Studio Art and a Minor in Art History. Shannon's interest in the macabre began while studying nature and the paranormal. The ethereal mood of her work reaches the extreme and addresses the taboo. Through her process, she explores natural and organic techniques used to imitate nature and discover Earth's imperfect beauty. Her use of stippling and cross hatching imitates the aesthetic of change through time. Watercolor, line and dot work assist the viewer to observe the Asian aesthetic Wabi Sabi, appreciation of imperfections.

Facebook: /shannonelizabethsart

Instagram: /shannonelizabethsart

Enakshi Johri
(Editor)

Enakshi is an educator, author and traveller. Her writings have appeared in *The Speaking Tree (Times of India)*, *Woman's Era, Alive, Infinithoughts, SivanaSpirit, Women's Web, EfictionIndia* and *Induswomanwriting*. Her stories and poems have been anthologized widely. She writes a weekly editorial, *Odds and Evens*, for a Social Journalism platform called *Different Truths*. She is also an eminent book reviewer and has been reviewing books for Penguin, Rupa, Hachette India and Half Baked Beans for more than half a decade. She has conceptualized and edited two books- *Unbounded Trajectories* and *Poison Ivy* (both available on Amazon). She won the *Most Influential Woman Award in 2020*. She has been featured by Kaalage, Bibliophiles of Bangalore and Indibloghub.com. She posts articles, essays, poetry and reviews on her website: http://aliveshadow.com

Facebook: /enakshijohri12

Instagram: /enakshijohri1